Weston

Also by Debra Kayn

Archer

Weston

DEBRA KAYN

FOREVER
YOURS

New York Boston

Forever Yours
Hachette Book Group
237 Park Avenue
New York, NY 10017
www.hachettebookgroup.com
www.twitter.com/foreverromance

First published as an ebook and as a print on demand edition: January 2014

Forever Yours is an imprint of Grand Central Publishing.
The Forever Yours name and logo are trademarks of Hachette Book Group, Inc.

The publisher is not responsible for websites (or their content) that are not owned by the publisher.

The Hachette Speakers Bureau provides a wide range of authors for speaking events. To find out more, go to www.hachettespeakersbureau.com or call (866) 376-6591.

ISBN: 978-1-4555-7712-5 (ebook edition)
ISBN: 978-1-4555-5093-7 (print on demand edition)

Wheels, Luke, Jake, and Jimmy (my guys in the garage): you're all hilarious. The way you act around cars, motorcycles, and grease is entertaining and a bit obsessive. Thanks for letting me invade your space. Totally badass, dudes.

Acknowledgments

There's something special about opening up an editorial letter and reading, "I absolutely fell in love with Tony and completely envisioned him as one of my crushes, Charlie Hunnam." From then on, I knew my editor would make Weston shine. Thank you, Latoya.

To my agent, Stephany Evans, who supports and guides me: thank you.

Weston

Chapter One

In an abandoned warehouse on Merchant Avenue, the warm stench of fear tickled Rocki's nose. Her stomach rolled, and she clamped her teeth to keep from gagging. She'd witnessed enough questionable dealings in the last four months of working undercover, trying to get the goods on Darrell Archer, but nothing had prepared her to watch a senseless beating.

Despite her revulsion of how business in the underground took place, hope soared inside her. Finally, Darrell trusted her enough to let her hang around while he took care of business. This was exactly what she needed because so far, she had nothing concrete to bring Darrell down and put him in prison for life.

Darrell's team, composed of four men, bigger and more evil than she could've ever imagined, dragged an unconscious man she only knew as Joe toward the exit. Joe, who hadn't paid his debt, foolishly thought he could outrun the underground drug lord.

"Come, Camilla." Darrell crooked his finger and walked past her toward the front of the building.

Going by her fake name, she followed him out of the building. She'd learned that jumping when he asked her to do something went easier on her and allowed her to stick beside him in her attempt to gather evidence. She wanted him locked in prison for a long, long, long time. The problem was the information she'd collected to date wasn't enough to take him down, and she couldn't escape and go back to her normal job of working cases until he went away for good.

In the backseat of Darrell's black Lexus, she buckled her seat belt, crossed her legs, and stared straight ahead. As his personal assistant, there were certain things he required of her.

Companionship, she could do. A specific job, she might not mind, depending on whether or not blood was involved. Today proved she wasn't up to witnessing a few hard punches to someone's face. The seriousness of the situation made it hard to keep believing poor Joe only suffered from a broken nose. She had no idea what would happen to him out of her line of sight.

Sex she definitely wouldn't do. Darrell had no reason to know that yet. He seemed to enjoy touching her hands and her arms, and giving her an occasional pat on the ass to get her moving out of the room when business was going down. She'd played it cool, and so far, he retreated when she became uncomfortable. Whether he understood her reluctance and disgust or he simply wasn't interested was anyone's guess.

Darrell, even at fifty-three years old, kept a steady stream of women coming and going in his life. Not all of them ran errands for him, unless you counted running to his bed whenever he snapped his fingers a chore. She suspected any woman who displeased him ended up on a ship out of the country and sold into the sex-slave business, but she hadn't gathered any proof. She just had a bad feeling.

Most of the women she'd seen were more than happy to hang around him. The black hair with a sprinkle of silver—not gray—peppered his temples, and the controlling attitude was a total turn-on to some women. Not her, though.

She'd give up the job, go into hiding, and start over somewhere else before she allowed herself to go there with him. However, she wasn't blind. There was something mysteriously charismatic about Darrell, and something equally dangerous. Those qualities made him unpredictable.

Darrell eyed her in the rearview mirror. "I have an assignment for you. In a few minutes, I'll be dropping you off near the corner of Main and Elm Street. There will be a red convertible Porsche with keys under the mat."

She blinked, keeping quiet. He'd tell her more or not, depending on how much he wanted her to know. The last time she interrupted, he'd locked her in the house for two days and forbid her to join him on business.

"The GPS is programmed. Follow the directions straight to your destination. A bar called Corner Pocket. When you're there, you'll take possession of the third pool table in the back. I want you to stay at the table all evening." He turned onto a side road. "You'll pay attention to the men, who will challenge you to a game. Drink, get loose, and I expect you to report to me tomorrow at noon."

"Noon?" She clamped her lips together, shocked she'd lost her cool.

That meant she'd have to find lodgings and enough time to call her mom without worry of someone overhearing or her fear of using a bugged phone. She gazed out the window to appear aloft to the plans. Four months, and Darrell hadn't trusted her away from his side. She slept in a spare bedroom, and when she wasn't with him, he kept her locked in the house under surveillance.

"I imagine at least one of the men will spend the evening vying for your attention. You'll be receptive to his advances as he'll want to get to know you better, and you will do whatever it takes to go home with him. If he wants sex, you will give him your best performance. You're to keep your ears open and bring back all information you learn, no matter how mundane you believe it is." Darrell pulled to the curb and left the engine idling. "I don't have to remind you not to mention your association with me or your true identity. You're a stranger traveling through town. I'll contact you tomorrow."

"Of course," she murmured, holding his gaze in the mirror.

"The car is across the road and down one block. Remember, you are disposable to me. Don't disappoint me…"

She nodded and opened the door. She knew her job, and hell to the no, she didn't want to end up like poor Joe back at the warehouse, who was probably resting in peace with the fish in the Pacific Ocean by now.

Darrell took off the moment the door shut. She stood on the sidewalk, getting her bearings. The area was familiar.

Bay City, Oregon, a half hour away from the police academy and the city of Cannon, where she worked on the police force and taught classes to those still in the academy while working her way up the ladder in the detective division. The youngest and only female on the squad, she expected the Archer case to take her to top detective when her supervisor, Detective Gino Marcelli, retired. Unless the special undercover job took longer and she failed in bringing in Darrell. Or Darrell killed her…God, she hoped not.

The streetlights flickered on, and she realized how long they'd dealt with business at the warehouse. They'd left Darrell's house before lunch. She crossed the two-lane street, anxious to start playing her role for the night. A public place would have enough people milling around that she could lift someone's phone and make a call home. She missed her mom terribly.

Her mother, the one constant person in her life, was the only parent she had after her dad left when Rocki was a baby. She gave credit to her mom for teaching her how to rely on herself and never depend on anyone.

Except lately, Rocki wondered if she went overboard on never admitting she needed someone else. Past boyfriends complained she lacked the gene to allow anyone into her life when really she was used to doing everything herself. That control was hard to give up in her personal and professional life.

She pushed her thoughts aside and hurried to the Porsche, which sat unlocked, top down, and looking sweeter than any ride she'd ever driven. She trailed her finger along the sleek side of the car, stopping at the door handle. Sliding into the tan leather driver's seat, she exhaled on a sigh. This sure beat her two-thousand-dollar used Honda Accord sitting idly in her garage.

Her chest tightened as she found the key, started the car, and put her seat belt on. She blinked away the pang of loneliness threatening to overcome her. For the first time since becoming Camilla Darrow, she wanted to leave the dirtiness behind and be herself.

Rocki Bangli.

Tonight, she'd go only by Rocki and enjoy answering to her own name. No one needed to know anything else. She couldn't take the chance of someone recognizing the odd-sounding last name, and asking around about her.

Five minutes later, she strolled into Corner Pocket, a quaint bar on the edge of town, half sports bar and half hangout, displaying the cheesiest neon-lighted sign behind the bar with a sexily clad mannequin straddling the letter C. She grinned and relaxed. The place was tacky and homey enough. She loved the bar instantly.

Whether it was the adrenaline of having time to herself away from Darrell or the scent of greasy fries and cold beer that brought out the fact she hadn't eaten since morning, she looked forward to tonight. She walked to the counter and slid onto a stool.

An older woman, hair teased out at least six inches on all sides, wearing a vibrant purple spandex yoga jacket lined with faux diamonds down the sleeve and making a wide swoop across the front, displaying a lot of cleavage, approached her. "I'm Charlene, hon. What can I get you?"

Unprepared for the night, she looked inside her purse and blew out her breath at seeing what Darrell had left her. Somehow, he'd loaded her with money, so she'd be able to eat and put a few dollars down on a game of pool if necessary. "A burger, everything but onions, fries, and a beer…lite."

The booming laughter coming from a woman who was no bigger than five feet five inches surprised her. She glanced behind her own shoulder, looking around the bar. She wasn't here to make friends, and the less she talked with the friendly woman, the better.

She found pool table three vacant, and turned back around. "Are there any rules on reserving one of the pool tables?"

"Nope." Charlene stuck the pen she'd used for writing the order in her hair. "If you play the game, you're responsible for the results."

"Ah, gotcha," she said. "I'll grab a table in the back."

"I'll bring your order out when it's up." Charlene paused. "Are you here alone, hon?"

She nodded. "Yes, I'm just passing through on my way down the coastline to California."

Charlene grinned, shaking her head in amusement. "I'll bet ten dollars that you won't be alone for long. You girls nowadays, I don't know why you force yourselves to be so independent. A good man by your side is a life perk."

She slid off the stool and watched Charlene walk away. Any other day, when she wasn't working for a notorious drug lord, she would've loved to sit down and strike up a conversation with the flashy woman. She bet Charlene was a kick, just her type of friend.

Remembering what she came for, she pivoted and headed toward the rear of the room. The third pool table remained empty, and she wondered how Darrell had known she'd be able to claim the table. Knowing him, he'd paid to have the area cleared and waiting for her.

Granted it was a Thursday evening, and in her experience most bars only brought in the crowds on Friday and Saturday. She moved one of the stray balls and sent it rolling to the other side. If there were more people in the bar, it'd be easier to find an abandoned phone lying around.

With no idea who the men were who would show up, or if they'd approach her, she picked out a cue stick from the stand on the wall. She'd played pool exactly twice before.

One time at her friend Gigi's house when she was a sophomore in high school, she learned a few things about the game of pool. She totally sucked, but had fun. Then she played it again at Cale Brown's retirement party from the sheriff's department. She sucked then too.

She rounded up all the balls and set them at the end of the table. She knew the basic rules. You hit the white ball into other balls, not letting it go in a hole. You called solids or stripes, and tried to beat your opponent by sinking all your balls in the corner and side pockets. On the player's last turn, you hit the black ball, winning the game.

She knew enough about pool to bluff her way through a game or two. Her stomach flip-flopped. She ignored the fact that the men she'd spend time with tonight were somehow connected to Darrell. She hoped they were innocent hits and her safety wasn't at risk. If they were business associates, she could be in more danger than if she was with Darrell back at the Crystal Palace.

A shrill scream penetrated the bar. She whirled, afraid a fight broke out. Away from Darrell, she'd have to rely on herself for protection. Anyone witnessing the precise movements of the way she fought would know she'd spent months training in physical combat.

Instead of danger, she watched a group of men stroll into the bar. Charlene hurried around the counter, heading straight toward them. Rocki leaned her hip against the table, struck by the jaw-dropping beautiful scene. The men were *hot*.

Three males, all different in looks but gorgeous just the same. The one leading the pack, dressed all in black with the coolest goatee trimmed close to the skin, yet dark and prominent, smiled. Her brows rose before she could stop herself. He knew the effect he had on women, she was sure of it.

The next guy to approach Charlene had warm brown hair, almost ginger in color, but not quite. He held his arms out wide and laughed heartily when Charlene smacked him on the chest and pushed him out of the way. She peered closer, wondering what had grabbed Charlene's attention, and spotted a woman tucked against the side of one of the men. Of course, she couldn't see the woman's face, but she had to-die-for waves in her blonde hair that Rocki would give anything to have in her straight black hair.

Dressed in jeans, suede boots, and a purple T-shirt with the words *Get Jacked* on the front, the woman left the man's side to allow Charlene to wrap her in a hug. The two women's mutual delight in seeing one another spoke of a close relationship, and their reactions fascinated her. She scraped her teeth over her bottom lip. She wouldn't call herself jealous.

She didn't know these people. Yet she envied what they appeared to have: a normalcy in their lives, a connection with others. Four long months of working undercover, without any contact with the real world, was apparently getting to her. She'd give anything to have five minutes on the phone with her mom to bolster her confidence. Even last week, she realized how much the guys at work helped her keep her head when working on a case, and that fact surprised her. She gazed away to check out the others.

Another man, more sexy than the others, with badass attitude, swaggered through the door and stopped behind the group. His expression warmed as he surveyed the people in front of him. He slapped the woman's gorgeous man on the shoulder, spoke to him, and then headed across the room. Aware of her staring, Rocki turned around and fiddled with the racked balls on the table. The last thing she needed to do was become distracted by a handsome face.

But she couldn't help it. The guy had it all.

Longish blond hair of multiple shades and tanned skin, as if he spent a lot of time outside. The size of his body gave him a toughness that belied his golden good looks. She couldn't help noticing the tight fit of his leather jacket, black Metallica T-shirt stretched across a broad chest, and jeans that—if she guessed right—had rubbed up against a few car engines in their lifetime. She'd always had a weakness for men who worked with their hands and weren't afraid to get dirty.

She lifted the triangle thingy, eyed the balls, and deemed the set up perfect. She stepped away from the table to set the racker back on the hanger and bumped into the man who'd grabbed her attention. The blond one. The tough one. The one who appeared a lot scarier up close than she would've suspected. Moreover, the intense way he looked at her didn't help set her at ease.

"Sorry," she mumbled, backing away.

His eyes softened. "You set the balls wrong."

"Excuse me?" she said.

"You need to rack them so the solids and stripes are beside each other, and put them behind this line." He slipped the triangle out of her hand. "Let me show you."

"Uh…okay." She gripped the pool stick with both hands and held on for dear life.

She had to get rid of him. At any moment she expected her targets to show up and challenge her to a game of pool. She glanced down at the man's boots and held her breath. Men who Darrell dealt with didn't look like caramel that'd melt in her mouth. Not this guy, who had too much sexy going on.

"Jumping the gun, bro," a male voice spoke behind her.

She looked over her shoulder and stepped a few feet away.

The other three men who'd come in, and the woman with them, stood nearby taking an interest in table three. Her gaze returned to the blond guy. *No way. No fricking way.*

"Just setting the table for the lady. It looks like we're out of luck tonight. She has dibs on the table." The man winked at her. "Name's Tony Weston. Yours?"

"Rocki Ba…just Rocki." She shuffled closer, shocked to discover these were the men Darrell wanted her to investigate, and fearful she wasn't up to the job. "You all can play, if you want. I don't mind."

"Right," he murmured. "We could make this interesting in exchange for sharing the table."

"Oh yeah?" She inhaled swiftly, wondering if he was in on the meeting and testing her. "What do you have in mind?"

Tony's grin turned into a genuine smile, and the effect wasn't lost on her. She felt the warmth all over, and she meant every little out-of-the-way, hidden spot on her body went suddenly hot. "One game. Winner calls."

"Calls anything?" She gulped.

He leaned in closer and whispered, "Anything."

Chapter Two

Tony stood beside Rocki at the pool table, and informed her how the guys from Beaumont Body Shop—a place where they apparently restored classic cars and ran a private investigation firm—always came to Corner Pocket and played pool on Thursdays. She swallowed her questions and smiled. Multidimensional men, every single one of them.

"The woman tagging along with us is Janie." Tony's smile softened and he lowered his voice. "Once she lets go of Kage and notices you, I'm sure she'll say hello."

For some reason it bothered her that another woman was around tonight. Dealing with these men alone was easier, faster, and more beneficial to her. She had experience with the opposite sex. Men composed ninety-five percent of the police force. She'd talked, listened, and used her female persuasion to her advantage on more than a few occasions. Women were sly, secretive, and a heck of a lot smarter. Janie would see right through her lies.

She had to wonder what Darrell wanted from them all. They were PIs. Not exactly men Darrell would do business with or hire. Unless he suspected they were casing him and wanted to learn more to keep the advantage on them.

"That's Lance McCray." Tony pointed.

She gave him a quick wave and grin. "Hey."

Lance's nearly black goatee wasn't the only impressive thing on the man. He had a sweet smile with full lips that she figured many women also noticed. She had to look away to keep from staring as he murmured a greeting. Nothing about him suggested he was anything but an upstanding citizen.

Tony leaned against the table, crossed his ankles, and said, "The guy beside Lance is Garrett Beaumont. Janie—who's lip-locked with Kage still—is his little sister."

Garrett, who had the same coloring and hair as his sister Janie, seemed to be the boss, yet none of the men were afraid of one-upping him or giving him a bad time about a woman named Sabrina. She peered around the group. There were no other woman on this side of bar, so Sabrina must be MIA.

"The guy next to Janie is Kage Archer," Tony said.

Her heart raced and a flush heated her cheeks when Tony mentioned the man's last name. She barely heard the introductions through the roar of her pulse pounding in her head. The picture of two months ago clicked into place.

The connection of why Darrell would want her to come to Corner Pocket, tonight, at table three, and meet these guys all made sense now. The uncle and nephew were estranged. She'd gathered that much from the paperwork and studying her subject before going undercover.

How could she not have recognized them when they came inside the bar? She'd delivered a cat to Darrell Archer's nephew's girlfriend—who she now knew as Janie—a few months ago. Back then, she'd thought they were a nameless, beautiful couple. Today, they were more. They were here, and being introduced to her. Their link with each other showed in every movement.

Kage, almost a spitting image of his uncle, with his dark hair, emotionless eyes, and disconnected personality, stared through her, but she knew he was taking every detail of her in, and not in a good way. She shivered, clasping her elbows in her hands.

Janie's shoulders rose and her chin came up. Kage's hand tightened around Janie's wrist, and an even scarier vibe rolled off him. He didn't so much as move a muscle or give away his thoughts in his expression, but she could feel the shield that came up in front of him, warning her to back off. Darrell was dangerous, but Kage freaked her way out. There was no doubt in her mind that if she moved too fast or said the wrong thing, he'd do anything to protect his girlfriend.

Unable to meet Janie's eyes, she continued watching Kage and murmured, "It's nice to meet you both."

"It's not the first time we've stood in front of each other." Janie planted her hands on her hips. "Unless you're pretending you don't work for Darrell Archer."

She glanced at Kage and moistened her lips, stalling. Darrell's nephew gave nothing away. He wore a mask of indifference, unlike his girlfriend, who was ready to take her down. "I…Not anymore. That was a mistake. I had no idea who he was at the time, and thought I was only hired to pet sit. How's your cat?"

"Bluff is none of your business." Janie's gaze narrowed. "Usually, I wouldn't ask what someone is doing here. It's really none of my business, but seeing as how I don't trust you and it looks like you came alone, it might be best if you leave before I tell Charlene who you work for and she throws you out of here. This is a clean establishment."

Rocki stiffened. "I—"

"It's okay, Rocki. You don't have to leave. Everyone is welcome at Corner Pocket." Tony moved in closer to her and directed his attention to Janie. "I think Kage wants to talk with you. Now."

"But she works for Darrell." Janie's brows came down and she widened her stance. "I won't have someone like her around Kage or—"

"Enough, Janie." Tony lifted his chin and looked at Kage. "Nothing's going on. We're here to play pool."

"Come on, baby, you're up first. Let's grab table two." Kage hooked the back of Janie's jeans and pulled her away.

Rocki watched them both walk a few feet away, wondering what they were thinking about her. She pressed her lips together and inhaled through her nose. She hated the charade. People were supposed to like her, trust her, and the absolute disgust coming from Janie hurt her more than she'd admit.

Usually she was someone other people came to for help. She dropped her gaze to the floor. She felt dirty and skanky being linked to Darrell.

Tony returned to her side, bumped her shoulder, and smiled at her. "Janie's a little temperamental. There's no problem with you hanging out here and shooting a game of pool."

She nodded, unsure if she believed him. "Just so you know...I don't work for Darrell. I did one job for him when he asked me to take care of a cat. I-I'm studying to be a vet's assistant, and when I was offered the job it was natural for me to babysit. I do it all the time for strays and pets going up for adoption."

"Okay." He studied her for a beat, and then motioned to the pool table. "Ladies first."

Unsure if she could pull off the gig Darrell sent her on, she hid her discomfort in the only way she knew how. She put a little extra wiggle in her step and tossed her hair over her shoulder.

It was one thing to work strangers. These people were friends with each other. Hell, one of them was Darrell's nephew. She'd have to put everything she had into her job and remain undercover, out of cover, and not blow her double covers.

Darrell must know Kage had hooked up with Janie, yet she assumed he'd sent her here to sleep with Kage. Kage was not the cheating kind. She'd stake her job on that fact, because the man couldn't take his eyes off his girlfriend. He barely glanced at her when Tony introduced her; he was that tuned into his girlfriend, who was willing to kick her out of the bar without any excuse.

She lined the cue ball to the corner of the table, shot, and broke the triangle of balls. The pockets around the table remained empty.

Tony chalked the end of his pool stick. "What brought you here tonight?"

"Dinner and a beer." She leaned against a nearby table. His question wasn't thrown at her for easy conversation. He investigated people like her for a living.

"Good place to come to relax. The atmosphere's the best in town." He tilted his head. "Usually, people come with a friend."

"Maybe my boyfriend is in the john, and I'm waiting for him to come back to play pool." She raised her brows, expectantly.

"There's no boyfriend," Tony said, sweeping his gaze down her body, his smile growing more confident.

She laughed. He seemed mighty pleased with his assessment. "Why didn't you let your friend Janie go after me with all the questions? She would've demanded answers and you could've found out more about me."

Okay, now she was being a bitch. She had to tamp down her act before she got herself caught. A fun game of friendly fire, trading insults, wasn't the best choice when she'd gone months without a relaxing conversation with a friend. But Tony wasn't a friend. He was her target.

She needed to keep his attention, because Darrell told her to go home with the man who paid her attention. She liked his attention. Even though she had a feeling it was scary Kage who Darrell meant for her to go home with tonight.

"Never had any use for being a gentleman, though." He grinned, leaned into the shot, and watched two of his balls sink into the side holes. "Solids." He glanced at her. "Working for Darrell and now eating dinner and playing pool with me. You've come a long way."

Tony continued to sink one ball in after another. She waited to reply. Not because she was feeling especially kind and letting him concentrate on his shots, but because she was using the time to come up with a plausible reason why she'd be here on this partic-ular night.

When Darrell prepared her earlier, she assumed no one would know her. Learning the connection between Darrell and his nephew and the investigators of Beaumont Body Shop put her in danger. Not for the first time in her career, she wondered if she was in over her head and should walk before she got herself into precarious trouble.

Tony missed the next shot after sinking four balls. He walked to-ward her, stopped, and without looking directly at her, said, "Are you in trouble?"

Damnit. She shook her head, probably too fast instead of playing it cool. His nearness frazzled her, and her stupid girly hormones smacked down all the training she'd put herself through to be the best detective she could be.

"You realize there are four people here who can protect you," he said. "If you're in trouble or need someone to help you get away from Darrell, we can help. We've done it before."

He saw too much. If she wasn't careful, she was going to blow her job. Therefore, she did the first thing that popped into her head.

She leaned in and put her hand on his forearm. "I'm only a girl who wanted to let loose for a change, play some pool, and have a couple of beers."

His brows lifted. "Yeah?"

She sucked in her bottom lip and dropped her gaze to his chest. "Yeah," she said on an exhale.

"Lucky for you, I'd like to see you get loose and play some pool, and I don't mind paying for a couple of beers either, so it looks like we've got a date, sweetheart." He turned and finally faced her. His mouth softened and the tension in his eyes eased away.

She melted, deciding she rather liked him looking at her. "Is that so?"

"Yeah." He inhaled deeply and appreciatively.

Hypnotized by the deep seductiveness of his voice, she looked at her hand touching his forearm. Her thumb caressed a tattoo of a full-length woman, naked except for a sash around her hips, inked in green. She wondered how and why he'd want what was commonly known to the PD as a prison tattoo, instead of the colorful ink tats popular with the legit.

Before she could ask him, Charlene's laughter broke them apart as she placed food on the table. Tony moved over and laid a big wet kiss on Charlene's cheek, leaving her giggling. He received a pinch on his ass in return.

"I can always count on you to make sure I eat," Tony said.

Charlene patted Tony's cheek. "I take care of my boys. I don't want you losing any muscle, because then I'd miss out on all these nice male bodies who strut around my bar every Thursday night. Besides, you've ordered the same thing every week for the last ten years or more."

"You're a doll." Tony tipped Charlene's chin. "And looking prettier every day."

"You're a sexy player, Tony Weston." Charlene shook her head as she walked away.

Tony, still laughing from Charlene's antics, removed Rocki's pool stick from her hands and set it on the pool table. "Let's take a break from the game and eat. Unless you want to forfeit…"

"Never," she said, sitting down and picking up her beer.

She drank a few swallows, set the mug on the table, and lifted it in the air again to drink some more. On the job, she never drank. However, to get through tonight, she'd need enough courage for what she needed to do.

The academy taught her how to investigate, how to interview, and how to play the calm nonjudgmental observer. They even drilled into her head that while undercover she had to do whatever needed to be done to fit in and save her position. There would be times when her moral beliefs and normal, legal behavior would be compromised in the name of bringing justice and peace to the community. She pressed her thighs together, catching the quiver between her legs. Tony tempted her to break her no-sex-for-sex's-sake law.

Casual relationships had no place at the police department, which made dating difficult. With her work schedule it wasn't easy to find time to indulge in flirting and building a relationship.

Now Darrell expected her to go home with a man, pretend to be interested in him, and God only knew what else. She swallowed her insecurities. Tonight would test her skills as an undercover detective. She was way out of her comfort zone, letting Tony believe she'd do anything he asked.

The plan she'd formulated in her head five minutes before walking in the door only worked if she pretended to drink too much.

What she lacked was how she was supposed to concentrate on her job, Darrell's orders, and the sexual attraction she felt toward Tony.

She had faith that once she left with someone, she could act out enough to claim she'd had too much alcohol and sleep on the couch with her jeans firmly zipped. A solid plan would buy her time to outsmart whichever guy asked her to go home with him, and it looked like Tony was the winner.

Then she could slip away early in the morning, fulfilling her obligation to Darrell, and still have time to gather herself before she reported in at noon. She lifted her mug again, and Tony's finger's circled her wrist.

"Easy, sweetheart." His thumb caressed the inside of her arm. "There's nothing to be nervous about. We're only shooting pool and getting to know each other better."

She let go and picked up her burger, lifting her shoulder and peeking at him while catching her bottom lip between her teeth. He saw everything. She had to stay aware and be prepared for anything.

"So, you're a private investigator and you pimp out cars." She took a bite, chewed, and continued. "How did those two careers happen?"

Tony continued eating and held up his finger to signal her to wait until he finished chewing. He wiped his mouth. Someone had taught him manners.

"The interest in working on cars was always there. I grew up with the guys you met. When we were young, we hung out at Garrett's pop's garage, learning all we could from him and dreaming about the day we'd work on our own cars. Kept us out of trouble and popular with the girls," he said.

"How so?" She popped a French fry in her mouth.

He flashed a grin. "Nothing makes a teenage boy more attractive to the girls than a muscle car."

"Ah." She leaned forward and tilted her head. "That's true. I looked at a few nice cars when I was a teenager."

He laughed. "I bet you did."

"What kind of car do you drive?" She wiped her mouth and leaned forward. "Is it hot?"

"It'd burn you, sweetheart." He winked. "A sixty-seven Camaro, midnight blue, twin white stripes on the hood with a three-eighty block and three on the floor."

She blinked and found herself panting. The description...meant nothing to her. The radiant way Tony's face came alive and his voice lowered to vibration levels left her panties damp. She wanted to see his car. She wanted to see him in his car. She wanted to see him doing her in his car.

She lifted her mug of beer and swallowed hard to get the liquid past the throbbing of her heart. "And the agency?"

"The PI stuff came during college. We all have our own reasons, but mine are purely selfish. The guys are my best friends, and it's all about keeping us together. I liked the idea of going into business with friends I trusted and knew had my back, no matter what happened, and I enjoy living in Bay City." He finished his burger. "What about you? Since you don't spend time doing Darrell's dirty work, what do you do to stay busy?"

It was a trap. *Think. Think. Think.*

"I do nails." She put her hands in her lap. "Only part-time. Luckily, my mom and I share a town house. It cuts down on expenses, while I go to college, um, part-time. I-I'm studying to be a veterinarian's assistant."

"And, that's why Darrell hired you? You're good with animals?" Tony leaned forward.

She reached for another fry. "Yeah, exactly. Love animals. All kinds, but especially cats."

He snagged her hand in midair. "I'm surprised a woman who paints other people's fingernails doesn't have time to do her own. Though I like them bare."

She ducked her chin. "Today was stressful. Just trying to decide between wearing mother-of-pearl or electric-blue polish seemed too tough of a decision to make after hearing how much it would cost to replace a…a timing belt on my car."

"Timing belt?"

She sat straighter, falling into the story. "Uh-huh. Life is good, but one expense and I feel like I should drop out of school and go to work full-time. I know it doesn't seem like the kind of pressure you're used to, chasing bad guys and trailing bond jumpers, but it's a job that pays the bills."

"Doing nails?"

"Oh no." She laughed to cover the lie. "Real estate."

"You're a licensed Realtor?"

"Yeah, well, I was before I started doing nails and going to school. I specialized in commercial properties mostly, but if a friend needs help securing a home in the area, I'll represent them. It brings in a little extra cash for school." She gazed down at her plate, shocked she'd eaten all her food while they were talking. "You don't need a new home, do you?"

He chuckled. "No. I have one that does the job of keeping the rain off me."

"That's good." She gazed past him.

His friends played pool, and seemed to get along while they threw challenges back and forth as if they competed against one another all the time. As Rocki watched, Janie caught her looking and glared. She turned away.

"Ready to finish the game?" he asked.

"Sure." She stood. "It's probably a good time to let you know, I've been going easy on you. You're ahead of me now, but it'd take nothing for me to clean the table in one turn."

He whistled. "Big talker."

"Hey, I only say what's true. I'm not bragging at all." She sashayed over and picked up both of their pool sticks.

She was going straight to hell. How many lies could she tell in a twenty-four-hour period and retain her aura of a trained professional? A pillar of society?

"Let's say we up the ante. Game?" He leaned against the table.

"You've already said winner gets anything. How much bigger does it get?"

He gripped the pool stick she held in her hand and pulled her closer. She stared into his eyes. Light blue eyes, so transparent she witnessed his pupils dilate.

"If I win, I'll be asking you to come home with me." He inched closer. His mouth hovered over her lips, not touching, but they shared a breath. "You'll say yes and get to ride in my car."

Holy shit. Darrell had sent her to check out Tony? She blinked. "The Camaro?"

"Yep," he murmured. "You in?"

"Depends." She inhaled, and held her breath. God, she so wanted in. "Can you deliver on such a big promise?"

He growled. With the ruckus in the bar, she would've missed the low vibration, but she actually felt the sound in the back of her fingers, where her hand pressed against him as she held the stick. The sensations coming from him swept through her body and settled deep in her lower belly.

"One night. In my bed," he whispered. "You come home with me, and I'll make sure I deliver."

She bit down on her lip, studying him. Finally, she whispered back, "Okay."

He stepped away and grinned. "Your play, sweetheart."

She moistened her lips and moved toward the table. Her hands shook, and she braced them against the edge, near the corner pocket. She wrinkled her nose, unable to focus on lining up her shot. She knew what Darrell expected of her, but she was unprepared for how smoothly Tony Weston could wrangle her into going to bed with him.

Usually, she loved competition. Even though she sucked at pool, she'd give it one hundred percent, because that's all she knew. As a result, she sent the cue ball straight into the side pocket.

Chapter Three

Tony parked the Camaro in front of the house. He opened the passenger door and held his hand out for Rocki. All the way home, he couldn't believe his good luck.

How many times over the past year, and almost constantly since two months ago, had he thought about Rocki? They'd never met, nor been introduced, but he'd lusted over her on two occasions while watching her work at the academy.

That's all it took. He knew it was crazy, the instant attraction, but damned if he could get her out of his head.

On both occasions, she had no clue he'd watched her while she taught a class out in the field. He'd planned to go back, introduce himself, and ask her out on a date. But life got busy for him.

First, there was the Hanson restore he personally brought into Beaumont Body Shop, then agency business took him out of town more times than he liked, and finally Janie came back to Bay City followed by her crazed ex-boyfriend, and all his time was spent keeping everyone he cared about safe. Business always came before pleasure.

And when he had free time, he knew by the devotion and skill with which Rocki conducted herself, she wasn't a woman you took out a couple of times or slept with and forgot. He wasn't ready to settle down. Once he tied himself to a woman, he'd have to settle in for life. There'd be no more cars, no late nights, and he'd probably have to bathe his dog once a week.

He gazed at Rocki. Damn…a woman like her would make the sacrifices worth it.

When he'd finally decided to make a move on Rocki, he saw her working with Darrell. He'd tried to rebuff his attraction to her right then and there, when she stepped out of Darrell's car and returned Janie's stolen cat at the beginning of summer. Though he'd put a halt to getting to know her, he couldn't stop the fantasies that played out in his mind. And now that he had her in the flesh, he couldn't help but slip his arm around her, settling his hand on her hip. She moved closer, bumping her side against him, and stayed beside him. He inhaled deeply, enjoying the pleasure of being next to her.

At five feet seven inches, she tucked perfectly against his six-foot-one frame. He glanced down and whistled softly. Though her body was slim and athletic, her breasts told a different story. She was made for loving. That's what threw him the first time he saw her, because she was not the typical hard-ass police officer he expected. She was soft, quiet, and beautiful.

She'd looked damn sexy holding a Glock as she was tonight wearing a slinky little T-shirt and tight jeans. More times than not, his fantasies veered in the direction of her wearing an evening gown and holding the weapon for some reason. Fuck, that was hot.

Tonight left him wondering what the hell was going on, besides his lust. She told more lies than a six-year-old boy caught peeing in the backyard.

He hated the fact that he knew she was a police detective. There were only two outcomes for tonight. Either she'd break his heart be-

cause she'd turned her back on her duty as an officer and worked for
Darrell, or she was that good at her job and she was working undercover for the good guys. Either way, her life was in danger and he
wanted to know why she was after him.

From everything he knew about Darrell, no police personnel
made it into the inner sanctions of the drug business. That meant
she'd done something no one else had done. The ramifications were
huge.

He unlocked the front door and paused. Once inside, he hoped
she'd loosen up and talk more. She'd grown quiet on the trip home,
but he blamed himself. It would hurt to have his illusion of the perfect woman tarnished if it turned out that she was on the wrong side.

If it had to do with Darrell, he'd bet his car that Kage was the one
Rocki was spying on. A burning sensation settled in his gut. She was
going to use him to get information on Kage.

Her obvious sign of zeroing him out today at the bar concerned
him on a different level. He needed to know if she was planning to
push herself into Kage's life. No matter what, he'd protect Kage to
the very end.

Tony kicked the front door closed, holding on to Rocki's hand.
He turned on the lights. Brute, his Saint Bernard, danced around his
legs.

"Don't let the dog bother you. He's harmless," Tony said.

Rocki gazed up at Tony. She was stunning, with black straight
hair, a golden tanned complexion, and an almost exotic slant to her
eyes. Everything about her set his heart racing.

"Maybe we should take a second to catch our breath," Rocki
whispered.

She'd lost her bravery on the drive to his house. Slowly, she'd retreated from conversation, keeping her gaze out the window and off
him. He'd given her space, not wanting to pressure her.

But the naked truth stared back at him now. His chest warmed. She wanted him. He'd waited too long to find out more about her, and what better way to do that than get naked?

"Don't think." He backed her up against the wall, planting his hands on each side of her head, and brushed his lips left to right against hers. "Need to kiss you."

"Um." She pulled away and licked her lips, but he followed her with his mouth.

The flick of her tongue connected with him and he growled before capturing her in a kiss. His body went solid. Fuck, she tasted good.

He held still, softening his lips, waiting for her. One, two, three seconds, and her body leaned into him and her head went back, giving him more room. Yeah, she wanted him.

Through her lies, her stories, her pathetic attempt at playing pool, she couldn't hide the one thing he wanted: her willingness. He'd dreamt of her too often, coming to him on her own, open and honest, giving him everything.

The tremor in her hands, the soft gasps, and shallow breathing when he leaned toward her weren't signs of a woman who wasn't actively participating in their flirtatious dance. The way her nipples hardened through her thin T-shirt did not lie.

She expected slow, and he gave her hard, possessive, and demanding. His tongue tangled with hers and his body pulsed. She accepted everything.

No, she couldn't lie about the attraction happening between them. Him and her, the feelings of wanting to get to know each other better.

He lifted his head a fraction of an inch and placed his forehead against hers. He inhaled deeply, enjoying the way her breathing matched his own. Hell, yeah, she felt the chemistry between them too.

The light from overhead allowed her to hide nothing from him. Her swollen lips, the heady emotions in her deep brown eyes, and the pulse beating at the base of her neck screamed that she was as turned on as he was.

Finally, he spoke. "You can say the word, and I'll take you back to your car. Or you can let me pick you up and carry you into my bedroom. Your call, sweetheart."

She raised her brows and stared at him. "I'm not sure…"

He whispered, "Sweetheart, you have to be positive."

"Wait." She shook her head and ducked under his arm. "Can you turn more lights on?"

He moved toward the door and hit the light switch for the living room, brightening up the area. "Better?"

"Yeah." She walked into his living room.

He stayed in the foyer, enjoying the sight of her in his house. Her lips moved, but whatever she was saying was in her own head and she wasn't sharing it with him. He gave her space.

She stopped, caught his gaze, and frowned. He leaned against the wall and crossed his arms, wondering how long it would take her to make a simple decision. It wasn't as if he'd asked her to solve third-world problems. It was sex.

He wanted her underneath him.

She wanted him, whether she knew that or not.

One more minute and he'd show her how much.

"You have a dog," she said.

He glanced down at Brute sitting on the floor. Brute's massive body leaned against his leg. "Yeah."

"He's adorable." She took a step toward him, and then another. "What's his name?"

"Brute," he said, letting her get away with changing the subject…for now.

His dog stood and looked at him, then bounded into the living room to discover his new play toy in the form of a real, live woman. Rocki shrieked in excitement and fell to her knees.

He would've laughed if he weren't still worried about whether she was going into the bedroom with him or not. He moved forward and snapped his fingers calling for Brute, but the dog ignored him.

"Look at his big, brown eyes. He's so cute and cuddly." She sat on the floor and pulled Brute's head onto her lap, hugging the dog's neck and rubbing her forehead between the dog's ears. "See…he's got teddy-bear eyes."

Tony held his laughter inside. Bloodshot, brown, and mentally aware, Brute's eyes were dog eyes, nothing more. At two hundred pounds, the dog was almost twice the size of Rocki.

"Come, Brute." He clicked his tongue. When Brute came within a few feet, he said, "Down."

Brute went back on his butt and sat. Tony moved forward, slipped his hands under Rocki's armpits and picked her up, until she stood in front of him. "Sweetheart, I like how you're enjoying my dog, but I want you paying that attention to me."

"Maybe I've changed my mind." She kept her gaze off him. "If you could let me use your phone, I'll call a taxi."

"No more games. No more using my dog as a distraction." He stepped forward, taking her with him. "I want all of your attention on me. Most of all, I want inside your head, because, sweetheart, you want me and I'm not understanding why you're playing me."

"What? Are you a package deal?" She glanced from him to Brute. "You're nothing alike. He minds well and seems to have more patience than his owner."

"Yeah, sweetheart. I'll give you that. You're making this hell on me by asking me to wait to have a taste of you and trying to distract what we came back here to do," he said, pushing her to tell him what the hell was going on. "But as much as I love Brute and think it's cute that you have no problem loving up on my dog, Brute's not the one asking you to come in the bedroom. I am."

"Do you think I can use your phone first? I promise it's not to call a taxi," she asked.

He pulled out his cell. She shook her head. "Your house phone."

"Seriously?" He looked to the ceiling, telling himself to cool down and hoping the blood returned to his legs, because he was hard, harder than he'd ever been. "Remind me to teach you about spontaneity."

She pulled her fingers through the back of her hair. "I'm sorry. It's really important, and I swear, when I'm done with my phone call, I'll go in the bedroom with you."

"There are cordless phones in the kitchen and in my bedroom," he said. "Take your pick."

"I'll go to the kitchen." She moved away from him and stopped. "Thanks. This means…everything. I'll make it up to you."

He slipped his finger into the neck of her shirt, and pulled her back to him. "Start now."

"What?"

He nuzzled her neck. "Make it up to me."

"I-I can do that." Her hands went to his stomach.

He kissed his way to her jawline, her cheek, and her nose, and hovered above her lips. "Waiting."

"Oh." She dove in and kissed him.

He laughed against her closed lips. She pulled away, frowning. The insulted look was adorable and for a moment, he felt bad for teasing her. Whatever game she played, he had no idea how one minute she was a sex goddess and the next left him wondering if no one had taught her how a man liked to be kissed. Instead of feeling turned off, he found her cute as hell.

"Go make your phone call. Through the walkway, turn left and the kitchen will be the first opening on the right. I left the range hood light on, but the main light switch is on the left as you enter." He kissed her quickly and motioned with his head. "Bedroom is down the hall in the opposite direction. Go past the rec room and it'll be on the left."

She nodded. "Okay."

He called Brute to his side and walked down the hallway, leaving Rocki to make her phone call in private. Brute trotted into the spare bedroom ahead of him, knowing the routine. He followed more slowly, checking to make sure there was still food and water in the bowls on the floor he'd left this afternoon. Normally, he gave Brute the run of the house, leaving the door to the garage open so he could use the custom-sized doggy door to the backyard when needed, but he'd trained Brute to stay in the room if he had company.

Although any adult could crawl through the flap out the back-door in the garage, Brute protected the place when Tony was gone. Brute had a hell of a growl, but only Tony knew he had more drool than bite. No wonder Rocki had bonded with his dog. He suspected she was putting on her own protective face when she really wanted to curl her legs around him and lick him to death.

Brute hopped up on the bed, lay down, and put his head on his crossed paws. Tony gave the dog a good scratch. "She's something else, huh?"

"*Woof.*"

He chuckled. "Yeah. She thinks you're cool too."

One more pat to Brute's head, and Tony left the room and closed the door. Silence greeted him in the hallway. Rocki must still be on the phone.

He strode into the bedroom, removed his boots, and stripped off his clothes before walking into the bathroom to shower. He'd give her privacy to make her call, and then he was going to make up for lost time. They'd already wasted an hour, and she wasn't even in his bed yet.

She'd made him work for every inch he'd made getting to know her, and still held the truth of what she was doing at Corner Pocket from him. He stepped under the water. Ninety-nine percent of the information she volunteered were lies. He held on to the one thing she couldn't fake: her attraction to him.

Whether she still worked for Darrell remained a concern, but that'd end after tonight whether she slept with him or not. He'd never let a vulnerable woman walk into the kind of trouble she'd find with Darrell.

She was hiding something, besides her real occupation. A few times, he wanted to mention how he knew she was lying, get it out in the open and deal with it, but he held back. There had to be a big reason behind why she'd concoct all the stories about what she did for a living, and he wanted to figure out the answer for himself first. Something wasn't adding up, and because he worried about how her involvement would touch Kage, he'd wait until she gave him something concrete. Then he'd confront her.

He toweled off, slipped on a pair of gym shorts, and walked out into the bedroom. The lights remained on, the bed still made, and he heard nothing coming from the other end of the house. Concerned Rocki slipped out while he showered, he went down the hall searching for her.

Before he entered the kitchen, he heard the way her voice warbled and stopped, staying out of sight.

"I'm safe for now." Her footsteps led her farther away, but her voice rose. "I can't tell you. You know that. I'm doing okay. I'm safe, so stop worrying."

He leaned against the wall. Going off her side of the conversation, he couldn't tell what kind of relationship she had with the other person on the phone.

"Hopefully it'll end soon, and things will go back to normal." She inhaled loudly and blew out her breath. "I know. I miss you too. Don't worry if you don't hear from me for a while. I got lucky and found a phone I can use, but now I have to go back to work, okay?"

His head came up and he peeked into the room. Rocki's back was to him and she rubbed the spot where her neck met her shoulder.

"I will," she whispered. "I love you too."

She disconnected the call and sank into the chair by the table. He studied the long line of her spine, the forward tilt of her head. Her shoulders shook, and his body tensed. She was crying.

He could handle an irate woman and enjoyed a good debate, but the soft sniffles of a woman's heart breaking left him incompetent and desperate. With no sister of his own, women were a mystery he loved discovering. Tears were his undoing. He wanted to fix whatever was bothering her, promise to get rid of whatever or whoever caused her pain, but if she was this upset over coming home with him, something else was going on.

His head went back and hit the wall. *Shit.*

The last thing he needed to do was emotionally tie himself to a woman in need. All he'd thought about since spotting her at the academy was how much he wanted her. Her quiet strength around the other officers set her apart from other women. Women who'd relied on him to make the simplest of choices…it never resulted in anything good. He needed fire and backbone in a woman.

He never expected to find someone like that so soon. When he wasn't doing investigative work, he spent hours at the garage fixing up classic cars. If he was honest, he liked being single.

He looked in on her again. She was hurting, and damned if he could hold himself back from helping her.

His plans for tonight fizzled like a shaken pop can opened too soon. He gave her a few moments, and when she failed to pull herself together, he walked into the kitchen. She sniffled, wiping her cheeks and hiding her face.

"Rocki?" He laid his hand on the back of her neck. "Everything okay?"

She cleared her throat. "I'm fine. Just give me a second."

Fine. He'd heard that word before. It definitely meant the complete opposite. Women had their own definition and, unfortunately, they kept the meaning secret from him.

"You're not fine." He squatted beside her chair, making her face him. "You know who I am. If you're in trouble or someone is upsetting you, I can make sure you stay safe and get the help you need."

She shook her head. "Don't…please."

"Sweetheart…" He cupped her face. "Trust me. I will protect you. All you have to do is say the word, and no one will touch you."

Her chin wobbled, and her eyes filled with tears. She shook her head, clamping her lips together. The pleading gaze was his undoing. He could no more force her to talk than turn her away when she cried.

"Shh, sweetheart. I've got you." He picked her up and cradled her in his arms.

Her face went to his neck, and she let the tears win. He simply held her as he walked to the bedroom.

He flipped the light switch off with his elbow, deposited her on the bed without letting go, and curled his body around hers. Her back to his front, he soothed her while absorbing her sobs.

Every time she gasped for more air and her body stiffened, he wanted to demand she tell him the truth. He could fix whatever problem she had. She only had to tell him, and he'd do anything to make her smile at him again.

He had no idea what the fuck was going on with her, and his first instinct was to call her superior and demand answers. There was a chance she was working double, playing both sides, with her badge on one side, Darrell on the other.

He questioned why he still found himself attracted to her, because someone who used people for their own good was someone he wouldn't want in his life. He ran his hand down the back of her head, murmuring words he'd had no idea he knew. His gut told him that she needed him and he wouldn't turn away from her yet.

A long time later, she quieted and fell asleep. He continued to lie with her, holding her, and keeping her safe. Whatever trouble she'd gotten herself into, he was going to make sure she sought help in the morning. Then he was going to find out why she'd lied to him.

Chapter Four

A soft snore startled Rocki awake. Her pulse raced and she blinked into the dark, trying to gain her bearings. She was at Tony's house, in his bed, and—she wiggled her toes inside her shoes—fully dressed. She laid her head back on the pillow, her heart pounding.

She peered at the nightstand. Four forty-five in the morning.

Tony snored lightly behind her. His arm thrown around her waist, holding her tight against his chest, seemed intimate and surprisingly wonderful. His legs bent in the crook of hers, cradling her body. She lifted his wrist, rolled, and slid out from his embrace. A shiver crawled along her spine at the loss of his body heat. She paused, kneeling on the floor, and counted to sixty.

Coming home with Tony last night was a huge mistake. Once she found out he was a private investigator and best friend to Kage, she should've called off her job. She could've lied to Darrell and kept Tony clean. Instead, she was helping bring Darrell's attention to a man she'd instantly respected for his career of choice and the way he stood up for her around Janie.

He'd gone out of his way twice to make sure she was okay. Then, instead of forcing himself on her, he'd taken her to bed to cuddle. No one needed to tell her that Tony was not a man who spent time in bed just holding a woman.

The soft snortles from Tony continued with every third inhale, and she closed her eyes briefly in relief. Then she crawled out of his room until she was halfway down the hall, and finally stood when there was no sign of Tony following her.

She paused, listening. A soft whine came from behind the closed door on her right. She laid her hand on the door and whispered, "It's okay, Brute. It's me."

When the dog stopped, she tiptoed the rest of the way. She had to get out of here before Tony found her missing from the bed and called her on the bet they'd made. It was unfair of her to play him for a fool. He was too smart, and Darrell had set her up. Using Tony and having sex with him crossed her personal line; undercover or not, she wasn't that type of woman.

She found her purse in the foyer. Being careful not to make any unnecessary noises, she slipped out the front door and walked away from Tony Weston. Half a block later, she slowed her pace and retrieved her cell from her purse. She bit the inside of her lip, debating whether to keep walking and bide herself more time or call Darrell right away.

She'd spent the night and fulfilled her job. If he asked, she could explain how Tony had to go to work and she left early. She thumped the phone against her forehead. Unless it was Kage who Darrell wanted her to sleep with, and in that case, Darrell was out of luck and she'd failed the orders. No woman would ever get between Janie and Kage.

If only she had a way home, and could spend a few hours with her mom without Darrell finding out. She stopped near the street corner. Using the phone to call her mom earlier at Tony's house had been a huge risk, but the chances of Darrell or one of his men tapping Tony's home phone were slim. She'd played it safe.

The emotional fallout from hearing her mom's voice hit her hard. They'd survived together after her dad left, and the years of scraping to put food on their table and a roof over their heads. Together, they'd both gone on to reach their goals.

Mary Bangli worked at Macy's as a supervisor in charge of displaying the women's clothing line while helping put Rocki through the academy. The only time she regretted her choice of career was last night. She gained no pleasure lying to Tony. Yet bringing Darrell to justice would earn her a solid seat among the male detectives and their respect if she succeeded in bringing down the infamous drug lord.

She couldn't screw up. Her life wasn't the only one on the line and depended on her succeeding on the case, and bringing Darrell to justice. She'd do whatever it took to keep her mom safe and out of line of Darrell's wrath if things turned ugly. Her mom meant the world to her.

Now Tony was involved indirectly because she'd failed to accomplish her orders to sleep with him. She gathered her hair to one side and rubbed the back of her neck. She'd gotten the best night's sleep she'd had in four months, but Darrell wasn't concerned about her stress level.

She glanced down the road toward Tony's house. She'd walked far enough. No longer in view of his place, she slowed down. Guilt forced her to look away. She'd expected him to act very differently.

He'd told her clearly they were going to have sex. She'd all but agreed, and then teased the man.

When he took her to bed and held her, letting her cry, she jumped at the comfort he offered. For a few short hours, all the stress from the last several months eased. The only thing she wanted was his big, strong arms holding her. He never questioned the reason behind her tears or belittled her for being weak.

He was the nicest guy she'd ever encountered. Ever.

What kind of man sent signals of wanting sex, yet supported her when she needed him most and ignored his own needs?

She already regretted meeting him. The timing was all wrong. Another place and a different situation, and she'd be all over him like cocoa butter.

A black Lexus pulled around the corner, crossed the lane, and slowed down. Rocki slipped the phone into her back pocket. Dread filled her.

The car stopped at the curb and the window came down. Darrell leaned toward the passenger seat. "Get in."

Panic seized. He knew. That was the only reason he'd known to find her out on the street this early in the morning, hours before her deadline.

Instead of running, fast and far away, or walking toward the car to hold on to the charade she played, her mind went to Tony. He was the kind of man she'd love to hang out with and get to know better. He'd never use his authority to make her witness beatings, drug deals, or, God help her, the blood of poor Joe without a last name.

"Camilla," Darrell said. "Get in the car."

She lifted her chin. As Camilla, she was trained to do her job. She moved toward the back door, but Darrell stopped her and told her to get in the front. She opened the door and slid into the passenger seat.

She remained silent, waiting, fearing what he would say to her. Did he know she'd never slept with Tony? Was Tony the intended hit or had she screwed up? God, she should've stayed at Tony's house until she had more time to come up with a different plan or at least time to call Gino.

Darrell gave her the forty-minute drive back to his house to contemplate her options, and she used his silence to her advantage. Asking Tony for help was out of the question and calling Gino and having him pull her off the undercover job would ruin all chances of her getting the lead detective's position when Gino retired, not to mention, make her take time off to lie low until they were sure Darrell wasn't coming back for her. The most she could do was continue her charade and hope he was lenient on her.

The sun peeked over the horizon as he pulled into the beach cottage along the pacific coastline. No one would suspect anything from the light blue shingles and white picket fence in a community of retirees and rental places. Even Darrell's men came during the daytime to keep suspicions to a minimum.

Darrell drove straight into the garage. He closed the door with the remote and waited until they were out of view of the neighbors before exiting the car. She hurried and followed him into the house.

He headed straight to his office, waiting for her to come inside, and then closed the door behind her. She stood until he motioned to the chair. He demanded obedience, and she'd learned her place months ago. Still, he forced her to wait to find out why he'd sought her out before her noon deadline.

She kept her gaze on the floor in front of his desk. Using her time, she blanked her mind, but the picture of Tony waking up and finding her gone plagued her. She dug her nails into the palm of her hand. She shouldn't care.

She had a night of flirting, played pool, and told lies. So many lies, she couldn't remember what she'd told him. Something about doing nails. She opened her hands and glanced down at her nails. No polish adorned the tips of her fingers. Tony knew, yet he let her believe in her babblings.

"Rocki?"

Her gaze lifted. She met Darrell's eyes and realized her mistake. She'd blown her cover.

Months of preparations and learning every aspect of the underground tossed in her face, because she forgot herself. She'd failed. Caught in the turmoil of what she'd done last night cost her everything. Tony made her remember, for a short time, she was still Rocki Bangli and not Camilla.

She straightened, hoping to cover her blunder. "Who?"

"Do you realize what I do to those who've broken my trust?" he whispered.

She shook her head slowly, opening her eyes wide. "I'm not sure I understand what—"

"Stop the bullshit." He stood and walked to the door. "You've put me in the position of doing damage control. In the meantime, you'll stay here. There are guards watching, and trust me, you do not want to try to escape. One phone call, one attempt at making contact with your superiors, one step outside the door, and my men will be on you before you can call for help."

She jumped out of the chair. "Wait!"

He paused with his hand on the doorknob. "I'd advise you to keep quiet, Ms. Bangli. From what I understand, your mother, Mary, has had a hard enough time in life. You do not want to cause more problems for her now that's she's on her feet, earning a nice living, and comfortable in the house you two share."

She clamped her lips together. *Shit. Shit. Shit.*

She slipped past him into the hallway and waited for him to lock his office door. He'd always forbidden her entry, unless he was inside. The rest of the house she knew was bugged with cameras, and his men would be notified immediately if she went outside. She'd tried before, claiming not to have known there were sensors at each door and window. She'd made it to the end of the driveway before two men had returned her to the house.

Exactly where his men stayed or how they watched her, she never found out.

In the living room, Darrell paused and faced her. He grabbed her chin and pressed her head back. "So disappointing, but you've served your purpose. I do believe my nephew will find you irresistible. I'm sure he won't let you suffer for long."

"Y-your nephew?" she said, fighting the urge to rip away from his touch.

He laughed. The sound, demonic and controlled, sent chills down her spine. "You don't think I knew who you were from the beginning? *Tsk. Tsk.* You for my nephew...It's a fair trade, I believe."

"You want Kage?" she whispered.

He let go of her and straightened his sleeves as if the act of touching her was distasteful and he wanted to brush her from his skin. "It's not a question of wanting him. I *have* him. He's blood."

Her gig was over. She stepped back. "You won't get away with this."

"I believe I already have." His mouth curved and she saw the enjoyment he got from having power over others.

"Someone will know I'm missing. My boss will—"

"Gino?" He smirked, but his eyes were cold and calculating. "Detective Gino Marcelli isn't the man you think he is. You were a toy in his game. This isn't the first time Gino has decided to go after his competition. We've been at war before. You think I'm scary, my dear?" He shook his head. "Deal with a man who hides behind a badge. With me, you know what you're up against, and I'm not going to play any games. I'm right here in the open."

She gasped, struggling to fill her depleted lungs with air. *No. No fricking way.* Gino was one of the good guys, a senior detective, and two years from retirement. "What are you saying?"

"I'm sure you can come up with your own conclusions, Ms. Bangli. A promising detective with your whole career in front of you, you'll figure out the truth eventually. So, you see, you have nowhere you can run to for help. You're mine, sweetheart... That's what Weston called you, isn't it?" He didn't wait for an answer, but strode away from her.

At the other end of the house, she heard a door close. She bent at the waist and braced herself on her knees. Her stomach spasmed. She was going to throw up. Gino, dirty? *Frick.*

Chapter Five

Tony pushed through the doors into the agency's control center at the body shop. He barely glanced at Lance and went directly to the back corner.

"Yo." Lance's feet came off the desk and landed on the floor as he ripped his earbuds out. "What's up?"

"Pull up whatever you can find on a woman named Rocki." He swung around his desk, hitting the power button on his computer, and sat. "Link her to Darrell and the police academy...She's a shield."

"The chick from last night at the bar?" Lance's fingers flew over the keyboard. "Personal or business?"

He scowled. "Business."

"Just checking," Lance mumbled, staring at the screen. "No one by the name of Rocki, with an *I* or *Y*, who has gone through the academy in the last ten years, is listed on the roster. I don't think she's older than thirty—"

"Twenty-eight," Tony said.

"Doesn't matter, I can't pull info out of my ass by age, but I've found a Rachel, Regina, Rochelle, and, bingo, a Raquel. Let me pull her up." Lance clicked the mouse. He pushed off the desk, and rolled his chair toward Tony. "Skip the deets, I want a picture."

Tony's hands suspended above the keys. "Bro..."

"Just do it."

An official photograph popped on screen. All Rocki's glorious, black hair pulled into a severe bun, her blue uniform buttoned to the neck, and a gold badge over her left pocket. He cussed under his breath. She was in deep shit.

"Call the rest of the guys in. We've got trouble." He stepped back to his desk and picked up the phone. He punched in the number for the direct line to Gino Marcelli's desk at the county office, located in the police academy's building.

"Marcelli," the voice on the phone said.

"Weston of Beaumont Body Shop and Agency here. You've got a problem." He sat and scrolled through the information Lance pulled up. "I need to know if Detective Bangli is working undercover."

"That's confidential information. I'm under no obligation to tell you what any of my detectives are doing at any given time," Gino said. "What's the problem?"

"Dammit. I know she is..." He rubbed his hand across his forehead. "She's working for Darrell Archer. I recognized her last night, not letting her know I already knew her identity and her relationship to the department. She slipped away early this morning. I normally wouldn't be concerned if a woman wanted to keep her private information to herself, but we had a run-in with Darrell a couple of months ago, and Rocki was working for him at the time."

"Sounds like you have girl problems. I suggest you drop the matter. If she wants to contact you, she will." Gino cleared his throat. "I'm walking into a meeting. If this involves police business..."

"Gino, you know me. Of course it's business. I wouldn't have called unless I believed her position was in danger. I'm going with my gut right now, and something tells me she's in trouble." He glanced at Lance, waved his hand in the air, and nodded when Lance pushed the record button. "Can you contact her?"

A lengthy pause came over the phone. "I'll talk with her, but I advise you to drop your interest in Detective Bangli, Weston. Now, I'm already late. I'm hanging up."

The phone went dead. He slapped the top of the desk. "Fuck."

"He's telling the truth. GPS shows him pulling into the academy now." Lance clicked the mouse. "Printing out all papers."

Procedures for someone undercover went beyond insider information. If Rocki went in, trying to bring Darrell down, Gino would cover her ass. Tony respected that. But something wasn't right. There had to be a way to get a message to her or convince Gino to get her the hell out of the underground.

Because she worked for Darrell, whether from the inside or outside, his attempt at getting information sent a red flag to their operation. Everyone knew his relationship with Kage. He'd take a bullet for him. Including doing whatever he had to do to protect Kage from his uncle.

The door swung open. Kage, Garrett, and Sabrina walked in. He stared at Garrett. Garrett knew better than to bring Sabrina in when business was going down.

Garrett shook his head, not saying a word. Kage lazily leaned against the counter, grinning.

Tony pointed at Sabrina. "What are you doing here?"

Sabrina Wilcox, Janie Beaumont's best friend and current pain in the ass to Garrett, strode to Garrett's desk, and jumped onto the top to sit. "Something exciting is happening and since I was visiting with Garrett at the house, I wanted to come too."

Garrett scowled. "We weren't visiting. You barged in and made yourself at home."

"Whatever." Sabrina shrugged and the slim gold necklace swung against her chest and disappeared under the scoop of her shirt. "You answered my question, twice—that's called visiting. I told you that you'd get better at talking with me if you loosen up. Someday, you'll be able to hold a whole conversation."

"Fucking seriously?" Tony glared at Garrett.

Sabrina's obsession over Garrett invaded on and off time. Hell, she was beginning to be a regular fixture around the body shop. Her antics often got her in trouble because she was too smart for her own good. She watched everything they did, and she was a powerful mediator when her heart was in it.

"You deal with her." Garrett crossed his arms. "Please."

Sabrina only smiled. "I'll be quiet. Besides, I'm waiting for Janie to come to the garage. We're going shopping. The Los Lobos are playing at Corner Pocket on Saturday. That calls for new chicker boots, and I've got my eye on a pair that's cray cool with a four-inch heel." She turned to Garrett. "Just wait until you see them."

"I already told you, I'm not going. I have to work Saturday." Garrett walked clear around his desk to his chair, keeping a wide path around from Sabrina. "Why don't you wait for Janie over at the house?"

Sabrina slid off the desk. "Real original, Garrett. If you want me to get lost, say it."

"Get lost," Garrett said.

She glared. "Just for that, I will leave, but I'm stealing your black Beaumont Body Shop T-shirt. The one with the silver writing."

"Why?" Garrett asked.

She shrugged. "You wouldn't understand."

"Sab…never mind." Garrett handed her his keys. "Only the T-shirt. Stay away from the rest of my clothes"

She grabbed the key ring and hurried out of the room. Tony stared after her, not sure what just happened.

"This is going to be fun," Lance said, grinning.

"Shut the hell up." Garrett threw an empty holster across the room, at which Lance ducked and came up laughing.

Kage remained quiet, his lips twitching. Tony tossed the top paper out of the printer onto the counter to get their attention.

"Rocki, from last night. She's a shield working for Darrell. I took her home after a game of pool. She slipped out of my bed this morning. I want backup to go underground and retrieve her." He looked at Kage. "You can stay out of it. I don't want you near your uncle."

Garrett strolled over and fingered through the rest of the papers. "Have you talked to her superior?"

"It's Gino Marcelli. He's not giving anything to me, as I expected, but said he'll make contact. But we all know if she's camouflaging as Darrell's assistant, he won't be able to without putting her life at risk and pulling her from the job," he said.

"What's she mean to you?" Kage pulled out his cell.

"It's not about what happened between us last night. Something wasn't right when I found her at our pool table at Corner Pocket, and I decided…hell, I took her home. You can't convince me someone connected with Darrell strolls into the bar wanting to play a game of pool at our table, at our time, lies about her connections, and goes home with me without hardly any argument, isn't under someone else's control." He unlocked his desk drawer and removed his gun and holster. "Then my night turned into holding her after she asked to use the house line while she bawled her eyes out. Nothing I said would get her to talk. Then she was gone."

"House line?" Lance ran his thumb and forefinger down the sides of his goatee. "Was she concerned about her calls being tapped?"

"That's the only conclusion I came up with, because I offered her my cell and she turned it down flat. The way she acted doesn't point to the behavior of a detective." He secured the strap along his ribs when his cell phone vibrated in his pocket. "She's scared to death and it shows."

He pulled out the cell and frowned. "What the hell? Someone's calling from my house." He clicked connect. "Yeah?"

"Tony, it's Rocki. I need your help." Her breath, heavy and fast, came over the phone and Brute barked in the background. "You're the only one I can trust."

"Sweetheart...slow down. Are you okay?" He pointed at Lance, flicked his finger, and nodded when the red light on the recorder came on.

"Yeah. No. I don't have much time. I need you to do me a favor," she said.

"What?"

"I need you to go to seven-two-six-four Appleton Way. It's out near Cannon. It's my mom's house. Her name's Mary Bangli. Tell her...tell her I said, 'teeter-totter, bread and water.' Then convince her to go with you. You'll need to take her to a hotel or somewhere safe. Make sure no one follows you. I'll pay you back as soon as I can. Please. This is important."

"Okay." He watched Lance, who nodded. "Got it."

"God. Thank you." She paused. "I broke your kitchen window to get in. I don't think Brute will get out. He's too big and he'd have to go over the sink. I swear I'll pay you back soon."

"Rocki, stay put." He slipped his pistol into his holster. "I'm on my way home now."

"I can't. It's not safe. He knows where you live," she whispered. "I'm sorry. I-I'll explain later when I can find somewhere else to call you. Please, make sure my mom's safe...and be careful. Watch yourself. I'll be in contact."

"Rocki, wait—"

She hung up.

"Dammit." He turned to Lance. "Did you get every word?"

"Yeah," Lance said, writing in his notebook.

"Pick up her mom, bring her to my house," he said. "Right now, I need to get both of them somewhere safe, and I can watch them better together."

"Got it." Lance grabbed his pistol, shoved it into the back of his jeans as he hurried toward the door. "I'll call when I've got Mrs. Bangli in the car."

Tony grabbed the papers off the counter, folded them twice, and shoved them into his pocket. His chest tightened. The fear in Rocki's voice, apparent over the phone, concerned him.

Garrett swept his keys off the desk. "Where are you going?"

"I'm going after Rocki. I need to find her before she moves too far away from my house. I don't know whether she drove or she's on foot." He kicked the edge of the desk and sent it skittering three feet. "What if she's hurt or this is a fucking setup?"

"What's your gut say?" Kage opened the door for him.

"She needs help." He paused beside Kage. "Get Janie, watch her. If Darrell's behind this…"

"Already called while you were on the phone," Kage said. "She's en route. I'll meet her at her car and escort her and Sabrina back into the agency. We'll wait to hear from you."

He met Kage's eyes. "Cover your back."

"Always," Kage muttered. "Go get the girl."

Whatever game Rocki played was officially over. Tony ran out to the back parking lot and slid into his Camaro. He pulled out and hit third gear by the time he straightened the car around and headed through town. He'd arrive home in five minutes tops if he hit both stoplights on the green.

After he received the right answers from Rocki, he'd make sure she and her mom stayed safe. Then he'd dig deeper to find out her involvement with Darrell. He clenched the steering wheel. As he turned the corner, his tires laid rubber on the asphalt. His gaze went to the side of the road. Rocki was a trained officer. She'd know how to stay out of sight. He only hoped in her panic, she slowed down so he could catch her.

He entered his street and locked the brakes. His car fishtailed and he pulled out of the turn and came to a stop. *Shit.*

Brute barreled down the sidewalk toward him, his head to the concrete and his tail down in concentration. He opened the door, but Brute lumbered right past him without lifting his nose. Not letting the dog go without him, he left his car at the curb and took off jogging after Brute. If he lucked out, his dog would have better tracking skills than he did and would find Rocki. Or he was screwed and Brute was chasing one of the damn cats in the neighborhood.

At the end of the block, Brute cut across the Lipskis' front yard. Tony jumped over the four-foot fence into the side yard in an attempt to gain some distance. Unable to see Brute, Tony vaulted the chain-link gate and hit the ground running through Doctor Jamison's backyard. Brute led him to the street behind his house, heading north.

Concerned that Brute decided to head back to the house and gave up on tracking Rocki, he slowed to a jog and scanned the area. Late mornings meant everyone in the neighborhood was gone to work. Garage doors were down, kids were absent, and no one loitered outside that he could question about seeing an unfamiliar woman in the area.

Brute barked and ran through the Carmichaels' side yard. Bob and Carla Carmichael shared a backyard with him. He rounded their house and spotted a pair of feminine legs, legs he'd noticed on more than one occasion, disappear through his kitchen window.

He slowed to a walk, checking himself. Going in there ready to wring her neck for hooking up with Darrell and putting Kage in the position to deal with his uncle would not get him any answers. Now that he was confident about what she did for a living and that she was safe, he was pissed. No woman should ever put herself in a position to answer to Darrell Archer. Cop or not.

Chapter Six

That big, lovable, stupid dog.

Rocki glanced at the window above the sink in Tony's house, the one she'd squeezed through to get inside, and couldn't imagine how Brute managed to get his massive body through the opening to follow her when she ran. Once she'd spotted Brute three blocks from Tony's, she'd backtracked her steps, dodging houses and cars, hoping the dog would follow her home.

Tony was going to kill her. She'd lost his dog. A dog the size of her fricking car.

"Oh my God. Oh my God. Oh my God." Rocki paced the kitchen, brushing broken glass off her hands and forearms.

Dots of blood pushed to the surface and trickled along the lines of her palms. She grimaced. Her hands stung, but she had to find Brute before a car hit him or, more likely, he hit a car and got hurt.

She rushed to the faucet and turned the water on. Holding her cuts under the stream, she scanned the backyard for Brute. She hoped the dog would return to the house on his own, but time was running out. She'd have to go back out and find him.

Nothing was going right. She barely escaped Darrell's men after she found the keys to the Porsche and broke all kinds of traffic laws to escape his house. Luckily, she lost the men chasing her when she entered the strip mall. Her knowledge that the ladies at Land's End kept the back door propped open to accept deliveries, thanks to investigating a burglary two years ago, allowed her to slip inside and hide until the coast was clear. Then she hailed a cab with the ten dollars she had stuffed in her pocket, and instead of having the driver drop her off at Tony's place, she'd walked two blocks making sure the area wasn't staked.

Now she was back at Tony's for the third time in twenty-four hours because she'd spotted his dog running away. Before she headed out to find Brute, she'd leave a note for Tony in case she failed. Maybe he'd know where Brute liked to run.

It killed her to rely on Tony for help. Until she knew more about Darrell's accusations of Gino working the other side of the fence, possibly working for the underground, she had to keep her mom safe. The only one on her side, or so she hoped, was Tony Weston.

"Dammit, Brute, where are you?" she muttered.

"*Woof.*"

She spun around, relief flooding her. Standing inside the house, in the kitchen's archway, was Brute…and Brute's owner.

A scowl marked his handsome face as he took her all in. She reached behind her and fumbled with the handle on the faucet to turn off the water, then curled her fingers to hide her injuries.

Tony pressed his lips firmly together until they all but disappeared. The usual softness in his gaze ceased to exist and instead he narrowed his eyes and pinned her where she stood. She gulped, pressing back against the counter. Even more frightening was the way his nostrils flared like those of a bull seeing red, getting ready to charge.

Her respite over Brute's return home fled and a new concern took shape. Not only had Tony caught up with her, but he was mad.

"Thank God, you found Brute." She shuffled sideways toward the sliding door. "He followed me, and I was trying to lead him back but he kept running. I thought if I came here again, he'd return. I-I'm sorry about the window."

He motioned toward the kitchen table. "Sit and start talking."

She glanced down at her hands, uncurled her fingers, and made to rub them against her shirt when he grasped her wrists. The gentleness in his touch put her at ease. He might be mad about the broken window and the temporary loss of Brute, but his anger didn't seem to be directed at her.

"You're hurt," he said.

"I'm okay."

"You're cut and bleeding. That's not okay." He stretched around her and yanked a handful of paper towels off the hanger. "Here. Put pressure on it."

"My mom." She stared up into his face. "You said—"

"Lance, one of the guys you met last night, who I work with, is on his way to your mom's house right now." He led her over to the table and kicked out a chair, sitting her down. "He'll bring your mom to my house, and you can see for yourself that she's okay."

She stiffened, shaking her head. "No, you can't do that. Darrell knows I was here and will come looking for me. You have to take my mom somewhere else. I'll pay you."

"I'll protect her." He placed his hands on her shoulders and kept her in the chair. "It's time you tell me what the fuck is going on, Detective Bangli."

She froze, knocked dumb by the use of her occupational title. She lowered her chin to her chest and stared at the table. Last night, she'd given him nothing to go on except the use of her first name.

Where had she screwed up? Darrell called her out, and now Tony knew who she was.

Maybe he was guessing, or he'd worked with Gino before and everyone knew about her going undercover. She couldn't trust him if that was the case. Darrell claimed Gino worked in the underground, and Tony worked with Kage Archer. Bay City was one big family with connections, and no one informed her how they were related beforehand. *Frick*.

She'd panicked in her hurry to make sure her mom remained safe and lost her focus. Last night Tony grilled her about her dealings with Darrell. His suspicions came the moment he spotted her at the pool table. But, exactly how close of a working situation did he have with Gino?

"I don't know why you're calling me by that name," she whispered. "I'm Rocki."

"Right. Mary Bangli, your mom, is on her way here now," he said. "You're messing your stories up, sweetheart. You've already told me."

She raised her gaze, willing to use anything to keep her mom safe. "Fine. I'm Detective Bangli, but please don't call the academy. I'm coming off a job and need time. The more people who get involved, the more danger I bring here. That includes you and the rest of the men from the body shop."

"I get that. I already knew who you were when we bumped into each other at Corner Pocket, because I've seen you before," he said.

"But, you—"

"Right." He tipped her face with his thumb under her chin. "I let you lie to me, but that ends now."

She sagged in the chair. "Everything is a mess, and I don't understand how it got this way in a matter of hours."

He concentrated on her hands, taking the towel and patting the cuts and inspecting them for glass. "What you don't understand is you're here with me. I'm not letting you run away to handle this on your own. If my guesses are right, I know the amount of danger you're in, and, sweetheart, it's not good. What I need to know is how you became involved with Darrell Archer and if your hit on me last night was in any way directed at Kage."

She shook her head. "I'm not sure why Darrell sent me to the bar. I only know he wanted me to meet the men who played on table three. You showed up. I was supposed to go home with whoever asked me…which turned out to be you."

"Why did you leave my bed this morning?"

She winced as he worked a sliver of glass out of her hand. The quick change of subject threw her. "What?"

"We've got two things going on. One, you're working for Darrell for some reason. Two, you can't deny that you came home with me on your own. It was not because Darrell ordered you to. First, I want to know why you left my bed." He held her wrists and made her stay in front of him. "Not why Detective Bangli left but Rocki, the woman I held all night and enjoyed the time I spent having my arms around her."

Holy crap. She stared into his eyes.

He wanted deep in her head. There was no time to discuss her lapse of judgment. Darrell could be at her mom's house now.

"I need to go." She tugged on her hands, but he held her in front of him.

"Answer me first," he said.

She pursed her lips and looked down at Brute, lying on the floor. "Did you train him yourself?"

"You're stalling," he muttered.

"No." She sighed. "I don't want to answer you. There's a differ-ence."

"We can either talk now in private or wait until your mom gets here and have her learn what is going on with you." He placed her hands in her lap, let go, and leaned back. "Your call."

She glared at him. For someone who would look more at home on a motorcycle than scoping out a cheating spouse for money, he had a weird way of interrogating someone.

"Fine. I left because I realized my mistake. I should've dropped my job when I found out who you were and what you did for a living. Once I heard you introduce Kage, I figured Darrell wanted me to sleep with his nephew. I don't know why, because anyone around him and his girlfriend knows that man hasn't looked at another woman in a very long time." She shrugged. "I wasn't going to sleep with you—"

"You would've slept with me," he said.

"Uh. No. I wouldn't have." She snorted, rolling her eyes.

"I could've had you at any time. Even at the bar." His gaze softened, and he looked damn pleased with himself.

"Dream on, big guy." She stood, walked over to the broken window, and cradled her hands together, wishing she could make a fist, but knew her cuts needed time to seal.

Tony was right. She'd fallen for his flirting at the bar. She'd let herself believe that their time together was real and not forced by someone else's hand. Four months of working under cover, and she never once forgot what she was doing.

She'd acted, played, and conned her way into Darrell's trust. Within a half hour of meeting Tony, she quivered in his presence wondering what it would be like to kiss him and fall into his strong arms again.

Not only had she failed going undercover, she'd failed on her date. "I screwed up," she whispered.

Tony joined her at the window and put his hands on her hips

from behind. She leaned back against him and closed her eyes, thankful for the strength of his body to help support her. She'd gotten in too deep. She hated to admit defeat, but she was in way over her head.

"I'll help you, but you're going to have to trust me." He kissed the top of her head. "To do that, you have to come clean with me. I need to know everything there is about Darrell and what his purpose is for having you contact me and the guys."

She swallowed hard. "It goes against procedures."

"Then you talk to Gino—"

"No." She trembled against him, glad when his hands slipped around her and pulled her hard against his chest. "Darrell told me before he locked me in his house that Gino's in his pocket. I can't go to the academy. I don't know who is telling me the truth."

"What do you mean?" he said.

"I don't know." She sighed. "Darrell never came straight out and accused Gino. He said I couldn't trust him, and that Gino worked against the underground, because he was working dirty and using the department for his own gain."

"Shit." He turned her around. "I called Gino and filled him in that you were with me last night and you left before I woke this morning. I wanted him to check in with you, in case you were in trouble. He knows you're running scared."

"If he's working with Darrell, he already knows I'm out and on my own." She let her head fall forward onto his chest. "I walk into the station and my life is over, like Joe with no last name."

He pushed her away without letting her go and forced her to look at him. "Joe?"

Her vision blurred and she blinked the tears dry. "I witnessed Darrell ordering his men to beat Joe—I don't know his last name. He'd fallen behind on a debt. Then they took him outside and there was nothing I could do to protect him without putting the operation at risk."

"Jesus…" He pulled her back against him. "You are with me twenty-four seven from here on out."

"My mom"—she blew out her breath—"needs protection. Once I have her safe, I'll take the next step in contacting the department."

"Don't worry about your mom. She'll stay here. When I can't look after her myself, one of the guys from the agency will be with her." He cupped her face and softly kissed her lips. "Do you trust me?"

She nodded. "I have no one else. I have to."

"Right." He chuckled and brushed the hair away from her eyes. "I guess that will do for now."

A knock came and Brute surged to his feet, giving one loud woof. She jolted, looking at Tony for reassurance that the person knocking on the door wasn't one of Darrell's thugs coming to kill her. Tony lifted a finger to his lips and stepped away, removing his pistol from his holster. He pointed to the wall. She moved in the ordered position, wishing she had her service revolver and a vest.

Alone in the kitchen, she looked for anything she could use as a weapon. She gazed around in morbid fascination. Tony was an organized man. He barely had the essentials on his countertops.

Without moving away from her post, she opened the two drawers nearby and almost squealed when she encountered a tray full of sharp knives. She couldn't outrun a bullet, but if she could get a surprise attack in, she'd cause enough damage with a blade to run away.

Whispers came from the other room. She flattened herself against the wall, the knife gripped at her side. She was naive to think she was safe in Tony's house.

"Rocki?" Tony called.

She bit the inside of her cheek. Even his people couldn't be trusted. Everyone seemed linked to Darrell Archer. A few bills, a favor, a marker was all it took for someone to turn against everything they believed in and do Darrell's dirty work.

She'd seen family men, businessmen, and even a priest meet with Darrell and walk out of the room with their heads down as if they'd sold their soul to the devil with no chance at redemption. She inhaled deeply and stood straighter. She'd have to protect herself and Tony.

She put her hand behind her back, holding the butcher knife out of sight, and stepped through the archway.

Her mom stood between Tony and Lance. Mom's perfectly arched brows creased and worry lines shadowed her eyes. Rocki sucked in a sob and hurried across the room, falling into her mother's arms.

"Oh God, I'm glad you're okay," Rocki whispered, hugging her mom tight to her chest.

Tony pried the knife from her grasp, a grin on his face as he handed the weapon to Lance, who shared a smile with him. They could make fun of her all they wanted for being paranoid, because they'd brought her mom to her.

Everyone was safe…for now.

Chapter Seven

The minute Rocki saw for herself that her mom was all right, she felt more in control. She opened the chamber on the revolver Tony handed her and breathed in a sigh of relief at once again having protection.

Tony not only brought her security knowing her mom had another set of eyes on her, he'd proven rock steady in trusting her decisions.

Rocki's mom's smile faded along with the red lipstick she always wore on her lips. At five feet, two inches, her mother appeared frail, but her inner strength shined through by the stubborn tilt of her chin and the short, chic hair she kept stark black with a bottle of dye every six weeks. Rocki nodded, trying to give her mom the strength to hang on and trust her.

She'd protected them both for years, and realized she probably did more harm than good in this situation. The more aware her mom was, the better on guard she'd be…maybe.

Confident in protecting herself, Rocki became vulnerable when the most important person in her life was also in danger. She had to think, and do it quickly.

"You'll be able to handle the size?" Tony asked.

"Yeah." She slipped the nine-millimeter into the waistband of her jeans. "Thanks."

"No problem." Tony handed a cup of coffee to Mary. "There's cream and sugar in the kitchen."

"Black's perfect." Her mother took the mug and patted Tony's hand. "Thank you for helping Rocki. I've been worried sick the last few months, thinking of my baby out there without anyone to help her."

Rocki stilled. "Mom…"

"What? I'm your mother. I worry." She looked over the rim of the cup. "But you have a nice, strong, good-looking man taking care of you now. Everything is going to be fine."

She glanced at Tony, saw amusement on his face, and sat down on the couch. The situation was not all right. Darrell would use any-one to get to her and keep her from turning in all the evidence she'd uncovered. "Listen, we're not here because everything went okay with—"

"She's right." Tony hooked his hand around Rocki's arm and hauled her off the couch. "You're safe here, Mary, and we'll let you relax."

"What are you doing?" Rocki asked, trying to pull away from him.

"I'm sure your mom doesn't want to be bored talking business. You're together again, and that's all that matters at the moment." Tony smiled at her mom. "If you'll excuse us, I'm going to debrief your daughter."

She scoffed. "Debrief?"

"Go ahead, Rocki. You two go about your civic duty. I'm going to unwind and drink my coffee." Her mother batted her eyes—yes, batted her eyes—at Tony. "Take your time."

Tony gazed at Rocki, full smile, loving the attention from her mom. She rolled her eyes, which only amused him more because he stepped so close their thighs brushed.

"Come on, sweetheart." He slipped his fingers into her hand.

Rocki allowed Tony to drag her down the hallway, only because she couldn't take the way he flirted with her mom to get her on his good side. At the bedroom door, she muttered, "Kill me. It'd be a lot faster."

Tony escorted her into the room, chuckling, and shut the door. She planted her fists on her hips. He obviously had no idea who he was working with, because no man, no private investigator, was going to take her case away from her, even if she needed his help. *She* would call the shots, and *he* would take direction from her. Besides, she couldn't have her mom fluttering her hand in his direction because he had a killer dimple in his left cheek. She was distracted enough without Tony pulling her thoughts from the problem they had on their hands right now.

"My mom needs to know the truth," she said.

He hooked her neck and pulled her forward. "In time."

His other hand went around her, low on her back, and pressed her against him. She shivered at the close contact. He'd touched her a lot since she'd broken into his house.

"What are you doing?" she said.

He stroked the side of her neck with his thumb. "Holding you."

"I can feel that." She sighed and let herself lean against him. "Why are you holding me?"

"It's nice," he whispered. "Go with it, sweetheart."

Something was odd about a man who could think about sex at such a dangerous time. Their lives were at stake and he wanted to cuddle.

"That's the difference between you and me. I have to work. I have Darrell after me, and my mom is in danger. I can't think about you or what you're doing to me." She looked away, trying to hide the fact that her body called her a liar. She loved the way it hummed when he touched her, and enjoyed leaning against him. He was tough, hard, and unyielding, and even through the stress of the situation, she was glad he was around.

She stayed within his embrace, unable to think of any reason big or important enough to push him away. She'd never had anyone who knew exactly what she needed. Not wanted, not desired, not craved, but simply needed. Right now, she needed him to hold her and let her know that she wasn't alone.

"What exactly is Darrell's plan for you?" he said.

"I don't know." She inhaled deeply and pushed against his stomach, distancing herself. "He locked me in his house, and I thought about breaking out the window—"

"Most people use the door," he mumbled.

"Yeah, well, my life seems to call for escapes…and enterings." She gathered her hair at the back of her neck and gazed at him. "Luckily, I found a spare garage door opener in one of the drawers in the kitchen. I still had the keys in my purse for the Porsche, so I stole it. His men came after me, but I was able to out run them when I hit Market Street and the outlet mall."

"Shit," he mumbled.

"I have proof Darrell called the shots underground. I've witnessed him ordering a beating and talking about deliveries of crates while at the Crystal Palace. I have the names of two of his men who picked up the shipments from the docks, which I never saw the contents of, but I believe it was heroin. They brought in a *tester* before the exchange. I can identify both men as working for and taking their orders from Darrell."

"Why didn't you leave when you had that much evidence?" Tony asked.

"I stayed undercover because I wanted more on him. What I have isn't enough to put him away for life. There are too many loopholes, and without solid evidence, they'd throw away the case. Darrell Archer is the only one I'm after." She lifted her chin. "He's the shark in the fishbowl…not the idiots he has working for him."

"Other men have tried and failed to take him down." He sat down on the bed and braced his elbows on his knees. "You've succeeded in staying with him longer than anyone I've heard of, and he won't stop until he gets rid of the threat. You."

"That's why I came to you. I want to make sure Mom's safe. But, she needs to know what we're dealing with and placating her will only encourage her to rely on you. I don't want her unprotected." She dropped her hands to her side. "You have to understand. Mom lives in a world full of glitter and decent people. Her biggest problem right now is how to battle the aphids on her tomato plants. She's a little…optimistic in her belief in other people. Somehow, I need to convince her how serious my problem is, so she can stay safe."

"No. She stays immune to what's going on." He shook his head. "The less she knows about the dangers, the better."

"How can you say that?" Her voice rose. "She's not your mother."

"Trust me."

She moved to leave, and he strode in front of her. She glared. "Get out of my way."

"Calm down," he said.

"Don't tell me to calm down." She planted her hands on his chest and pushed. He widened his stance, and she dodged to the left, failing in her escape. "Let go of me."

He twirled her around, manipulating her as if she were a puppet. "You asked for my help. Now, trust me."

"I don't trust anyone." She snorted to prove her point.

His lips twitched right before he lowered his head. His mouth skimmed hers. "You're so damn addictive."

She clamped her lips shut. He laughed against her mouth. There was something incredibly seductive about the way his lips softened and his breath filled her space. She closed her eyes, so he wouldn't see her resolve to stay angry with him weaken.

"I'll never get enough of you." He rubbed his nose against hers. "Ever."

She stretched to her tiptoes, wanting to hear more about how much he wanted her.

"You"—he nibbled the corner of her lips—"taste fucking great."

She wound her arms around his neck and pulled him down, capturing the kiss. He took what she offered, nudging, licking, and nipping her lips until her spine quivered. She opened her mouth and moaned as his tongue touched hers. *Holy fricktastic.*

She raised her leg and ran her thigh against his jeans. He pulled back, gasping, his gaze heated. She tugged, not ready to stop, but his body went hard as he gazed off to the side.

"What?" She hated the whine in her voice, but she wanted to keep kissing him.

"Shh." He set her away from him.

The fog of lust Tony had created vanished, and she heard voices coming from somewhere in the house. Her pulse thrummed faster. She removed her pistol and stepped forward. Tony held up his hand, hitched his thumb toward the doorway to let her know where the noise came from, and then scissor-walked his two fingers in front of him to signal he would go alone to case the house. She rolled her eyes. He wasn't going to leave her behind to hide away in the bedroom.

"It's my mom out there in the living room with whoever just walked into your house," she whispered. "I'm going too."

He leaned closer. "Trust me, sweetheart."

God, she hated when a civilian pulled rank—not that she'd ever had one try. She followed him out of the bedroom and down the hall. He glanced over his shoulder once he looked into the living room, and put his weapon in his holster. She did not.

He could go on believing he had control of the situation, but she knew firsthand what Darrell was capable of doing when someone put his guard down. At this point and after this many hours, Darrell could have anyone on his payroll, even Kage or one of Tony's ex-girlfriends. She kept her gun raised to her chest and skirted the wall as Tony walked out into the living room without any worries.

She slid to the opposite side, peeked into the room, and frowned.

An older woman with her dark blonde hair in a long braid dangling down her back, wearing jeans and a red T-shirt with the word *Vegas* in glitter, stood with her arm wrapped around Rocki's mom. Both women whispered to each other, wearing concerned looks. Tony slapped the man in the room on the back and got pulled into a hug before they both grinned at each other and separated. A man who now stared at her with startling transparent blue eyes that matched Tony's. She lowered the pistol and slid it back into her jeans.

The man's eyes crinkled at the corners as he stepped past Tony, a slight limp to his walk. "I'm Caleb. You must be Rocki."

She nodded. "Yes, sir."

"There she is." The woman with her mom rushed forward and hugged Rocki. "I'm Pauline, Tony's mom."

She leaned back, taken by surprise. "Um, it's nice to meet you, ma'am."

"Isn't she adorable?" Pauline held Rocki by the shoulders and tilted her head to the side, either sizing her up or soaking her in, Rocki wasn't sure. "Please, call us Caleb and Pauline."

"Okay." She escaped and moved over to her mother.

Tony joined her and put his arm around her waist. She scooted closer to her Mary, but Tony tugged her tight against him. *What the…?*

"Oh my…" Pauline elbowed Caleb. "This is wonderful. We had no idea when we decided to drive up from Vegas and spend time with you before heading home that we'd get to meet your girlfriend and her mother. This calls for a celebration. We'll take you out to dinner. How does the Crystal Palace sound to everyone?"

"No!" Rocki and Tony answered at the same moment.

Chapter Eight

Mom and Dad sat together on the couch. Mary sat in the recliner with Rocki perched on the arm of the chair, holding her mom's hand. He leaned against the fireplace, uncomfortable with the direction the conversation headed.

Without a chance to make sure Mary only knew enough information about the Archer case, Tony's mom forged straight into discussing their current problem. He gritted his teeth together. The questions kept coming, one after another.

He stood firm. "This is a bad idea."

"Sorry, son. I agree with Pauline. If Mary and Rocki are in trouble, the more eyes on them, the better. It's our duty as your parents to help keep your woman safe. She's part of the family, son. It's no different from if we were going to war. A man goes down, we all go down with him." His dad pulled out his cell phone.

"Who are you calling?" he asked, hoping like hell it wasn't some of his father's war buddies. That was all he needed to deal with on top of Darrell.

"I'm ordering pizza." Dad gazed across the room. "Pepperoni, sausage, and mushrooms?"

"Tomatoes too? Rocki loves fresh tomatoes." Mary sat straighter in the chair. "It'll be like a celebration. We'll concentrate on all the good things happening, and push this Darrell person out of our minds for the night."

Tony looked at Rocki and willed her to take control over her mom. She shrugged, and almost seemed happy with the change of plans. Probably because his parents were publicly executing him, and he was useless to stop them.

He loved his parents, but…shit. He did not need them here right now.

"Dad." Tony walked over and sat on the coffee table, facing his father on the couch. "You need to listen to me. This is serious. We have no wiggle room here. Rocki and Mary must stay under watch continually. I can't have people walking up to my door. That includes having deliveries brought to the house, or having you take Mary shopping or to the Crystal Palace."

"It's pizza, son." He stood and clapped Tony on the shoulder. "Unless the guy you're after is a pimply faced eighteen-year-old wearing an ugly checkered shirt and carrying a couple cardboard pizza boxes, we're safe."

Tony stood and growled. "Dad. Kitchen. Now."

"Anthony…" his dad said. He chose to ignore the warning in his father's tone.

Tony lifted his chin and nodded toward the other room. Caleb's mouth tightened, but he returned the nod and kept his mouth shut. He walked out of the room and, thankfully, his dad followed.

In the privacy of the kitchen, he counted to five, and laid down the law. "This stays between you and me."

"Okay, son," his dad said.

"We're not messing around with a crazy drug addict. The man who is after them is cold, calculating, and smart. He's also powerful.

Everyone who stays here is putting their life on the line. Are you getting me?"

His dad nodded, lowering his brows. "Got it."

"Now, I need you to do me a favor. Go back in the other room and suggest to Mom and Rocki's Mom that you've changed your mind. Then take both of them to the airport and fly to wherever the hell you want. I'll have the guys from the agency escort you the entire way and stay until the plane takes off. I'll foot the bill. You'll stay there with them until I call you. Understand?"

His dad leaned closer. "You're serious about this guy putting their lives in danger."

"Fuck, yeah," he said. "I don't want you or mom involved, and Mary needs to stay away from Bay City until we can get some answers."

"What about Rocki?" Dad asked. "Is she in danger?"

"I'll protect Rocki."

A loud, deep sigh of acceptance came from his dad. "Hell, son, why didn't you say you meant business?"

He'd explained the situation in more ways than he thought possible, but his parents and Mary's mom were too caught up in seeing him and Rocki together. He removed his wallet and extracted a credit card. "Go straight to the airport. Buy the clothes you need once you arrive at your destination."

His dad pushed his hand away. "No way. I'll pay for the women and keep them safe. I was in charge of a whole barrack. I can manage overseeing two women."

Having grown up under his dad's roof, and having similar thoughts on what was right and wrong, Tony put his wallet in his pocket. His dad had pride and served his country, powered through having his thigh shattered and reconstructed, and never once lay down and admitted defeat. If anyone could keep his mother and

Mary safe while they were out of the area, it was his dad.

He shook his father's hand, pulling him into a shoulder tap. "Hawaii's nice this time of year, yeah?"

"Right." His dad held Tony's face and brought his forehead to his. "Stay clean. Keep that girl safe. She's a good one, son. The kind of woman you'd wake up every morning with and hope to get to know everything about in your lifetime."

"I hear you," he said. "Thanks, Dad. I owe you."

"Never, boy, never." His dad slapped him on the shoulder, squeezed, and left the rest unsaid.

Tony understood. Growing up, both his parents gave him their one hundred percent support in whatever he did, whether he was right or wrong in his decisions. He knew his place as their son would never waver. They gave him enough freedom to get into trouble, and the tools to work his way out.

He walked back into the living room, sought out Rocki, and gave her a wink. He grinned when she visibly relaxed. He'd never get used to how she tuned in to him, even when they didn't see eye to eye.

"All right, change of plans. We're going to make this situation easier on Tony and Rocki. The kids need space and time to bring their lives under control so they can get on with real things." His dad clapped his hands. "How would you two beautiful ladies like to catch a flight to Hawaii and bask in the sun?"

Tony's mom squealed and rushed toward his dad. Mary looked at Rocki and frowned. He moved forward, wanting to assure Mary he'd take care of her daughter and, in turn, nothing would happen to her.

"Tony?" Rocki whispered, distracting him. "What's going on?"

"Vacation time, sweetheart." He grasped her hand and pulled her onto her feet. "Your mom will be fine and better protected away from Bay City. You'll be safe here with me and the guys watching over you. When we have everything settled, your mom will come back and life will return to normal. In the meantime, my dad will watch over her. She'll be fine."

"I think I should stay with Rocki." Mary worked her lips in worry. "I don't even know your parents…"

"It'll be the perfect time for you all to get to know each other." Tony lowered his voice. "I understand you want to stay with your daughter, but I can assure you, she's perfectly safe, between me and the other three private investigators at the body shop, plus your daughter is trained and knows how to handle herself in this type of situation. She'll be safe and protected staying at the house with me. It would help Rocki to know you're somewhere safe too, and will let her concentrate on her job."

His mom walked over and slipped her arm around Mary's shoulders. "It'll be fine. Caleb will make sure we're safe and I have all the faith in my son to keep Rocki protected. If you come with us, it'll be one less worry for your daughter. You don't want to make the case more difficult for her. She needs to concentrate and bring down the bad guy."

Mary studied Rocki, concern evident in the way her brow wrinkled and she pursed her lips. "How long will we be gone? I'll need to call work and take vacation time."

"Let's count on one week for now." Tony turned to Rocki and whispered, "Why don't you show her where the phone is in the kitchen. Make sure she doesn't tell anyone where they're headed…for now."

After the phone calls were made, their parents herded into the car and headed to the airport. Tony sat down on the couch and used the cordless phone to call Lance. In quick order, he scheduled a new window and a top-of-the-line security system for installation in the house within the hour. Only one matter remained, and he'd cover how to handle Darrell when everyone arrived.

"Rocki?" he called.

She walked to the bedroom after saying good-bye to her mom, and while he kept an eye out for her to make sure she remained in the house, he finished the business that needed taken care of before they could proceed. He strode down the hallway. She'd gone through a lot today, and he wouldn't be surprised to find her falling apart.

Instead, he found her curled on his bed, her arms wrapped around Brute, and her head buried in the dog's fur. He leaned against the door frame, taking the time to soak in having her in his home, lying in his bed. How many times had he fantasized in the last year about her being here, and about getting to know the woman who held a Glock with steel reserve while blowing a hole in every target. He inhaled deeply. She'd hypnotized him with her quiet strength in a tight package that could've done centerfolds in any men's magazine.

He knew then that to get close to Rocki, he'd have to play smart and bide his time. She wasn't like the women he usually went out with. She was smart and strong, and deserved someone steady in her life. He wasn't sure if he was ready to tie himself down.

Although it felt nice to be needed, he had to let her take the lead on Darrell. He wasn't sure he could step back, because when it came to Kage's uncle, Tony would do anything to protect Kage and Rocki from dealing with the drug lord.

Brute lifted his head and gave Tony his sweet dog look. He harrumphed. Damn dog. Brute knew the rules. Tony only allowed him to lie on the bed in the spare bedroom.

Yet he let Brute lie beside Rocki. She obviously wanted and needed his dog's company. For how much he wanted her curled around him, taking his comfort, his safety, his warmth, he wouldn't deny her the simple act of liking his dog.

She'd gone through a lot, fighting her way out of Darrell's house. Hell, she'd been deeper into the underground than any other shield, and he admired her tenacity. Even Kage, the nephew of the drug lord, knew of no one who'd gone underground and walked away unscathed. Every meeting between Kage and his uncle happened in a designated spot, away from Darrell's business.

He had no idea how she'd pulled her job off. His chest warmed. Any man looking at her would see her and decide she was special. Someone to protect, cherish, and pamper. He'd give all his attention to her in an attempt to get a fraction of her responsiveness back. She was what men created dreams out of, and part of him was afraid she'd *poof* into thin air if he failed in his job to take care of her.

He'd never make such a mistake. He'd hold on tight and remind her every day of how much he wanted to love on her. He'd make her happy and in return, she'd make him the luckiest son of a bitch in town.

His phone vibrated in his pocket. He fished it out of his jeans and gazed down at the screen. The guys were here.

He closed the bedroom door, leaving it cracked open in case Brute needed out. It was probably best that Rocki was asleep. He could get down to business with the guys, fill them in, and plan their next step on how to deal with Darrell. When Rocki woke up, he'd go over the new plans. One less thing for her to stress out about was top priority today.

He walked into the living room and through the front window spotted Kage's Mustang, Lance's Harley, and Garrett's Cuda pulling into the driveway, one after another. The neighbors would think nothing of the flash of cars at his house, since the guys routinely played poker one day a week at the house, depending on everyone's schedule. Even the afternoon hours weren't a strange time to get together.

If Darrell's men were watching, they'd soon realize they weren't dealing with only Rocki. The Beaumont Body Shop guys were now involved and would do anything to protect her.

He opened the door. "Hey. Everything go okay at the airport?"

"No problems. Not even a tail." Garrett hitched his thumb behind him. "I brought Swanson to do the security system."

"Good." He lifted his chin at Swanson. "You can enter the garage through the kitchen. I want all entrances monitored, including the windows. Make sure to seal the dog flap at the back door in the garage tight and put a wire on it. Brute will have to deal with staying in the house while I'm pulled away from home."

Kage walked in carrying a small window. "Lance...your turn replacing the window. I made the last repair."

"Right," Lance muttered, taking the glass piece and walking toward the kitchen. "Hey, Weston, where are your tools?"

"Garage," he said, grinning at Kage. "By the way, you did not do the last repair. I fixed the McKenzies' back door when we went after Jackson for jumping bail."

Kage shrugged. "You know that. I know that. Lance knows nothing."

"I heard that, asshole," Lance yelled from the other room.

He chuckled, pointing Kage into the living room. "We need to talk."

"Figured." Kage walked over and plopped into the recliner. "Just to let you know, I haven't had any contact with Uncle Darrell since Janie returned the money she stole eight weeks ago."

"I know," he said, taking a spot on the couch. "I need your advice on how to go forward. We both know he won't stop coming after Rocki. He knows she's a shield, and will want to stop any information from getting out that she's collected while working for him. I need to know how we can work with him."

"Work?" Kage shook his head. "Uncle Darrell is not going to do you a favor and let her walk away. That's not how he prefers to do business. Even if she swears to him that she'll keep his secrets, he won't risk her coming after him. She's a liability, a threat to everything he encompasses. Maybe—and that's a huge fucking maybe—if she weren't on the force, he'd risk waiting and seeing what she's going to do. But he won't let this go without seeking revenge. He'll keep her under watch and wait for a time to get rid of her. He knows she wants him put away for life…What do you think he'll do?"

"Right." He leaned forward and braced his elbows on his knees. "She won't quit. Being a detective is her life, and she's damn good at what she does. She lasted four months before being caught, and you know how tough that is."

"Yeah." Kage folded his hands over his abdomen. "What are you thinking?"

"I'm going to go after him," he said. "I'll keep him busy and his attention off Rocki, until she can contact her superior and have the squad watching her back."

Kage stared at him a few beats. "I'm in."

"Hell, no. You're staying away from Darrell." He stood and strolled across the living room, stopping at the fireplace. He leaned his elbow against the hearth. "I'm going alone. You have Janie to think about now. I wouldn't put you in the position to deal with your uncle or link him to you more than he already is by blood. You've worked too fucking hard to stay clear of him."

"Already there, bro. It's family." Kage clasped his hands behind his head. "The only way you'd be able to step away from Uncle Darrell is to hand over your girl or distract him by handing me over in exchange."

That wasn't going to happen. Even if Rocki meant nothing to him, he'd never willingly let any woman walk into the underground or hand her personally to Darrell. He dropped his chin and stared at his boot. Kage would never let him go in alone, but putting him into contact with his uncle would personally kill Kage.

Not much fazed his friend, but he walked on the right side of the law. His need to remain untouched by the Archer name bore deeply into his soul. Even if no one found out Kage had entered his uncle's territory, Kage's guilt over his own involvement would eat away at him.

"I'll go back in," Rocki said from behind him.

His gaze snapped to hers. She stood at the entrance to the living room, her clothes wrinkled, and lines from her hand imprinted on her cheek. Her midnight-black hair lay messily around her shoulders. His chest tightened as he wished he had time to take in the warm, sleepy Rocki. Rocki, who was in his bed moments ago with his dog. Rocki, who had bigger balls than most men.

She wasn't going back to Darrell.

Despite her skill and dedication of taking care of herself, she was his responsibility. So he said the first thing that popped into his head. "Hell, no."

Chapter Nine

For the first time in months, Rocki spent time alone without worrying about who was watching. She studied Tony's living room. But her comfort was all an illusion, because despite how safe she felt with Tony, she had to catch Darrell before she could really relax.

She'd gone over every move she'd made while staying with Darrell, and still couldn't figure out how she'd given herself away. She crossed her arms and cupped her elbows in her hands. God, maybe she was going crazy. Drug deals, weapons bandied about in public, money exchanged, her every moment watched by either people working for Darrell or cameras aimed on her room.

Four months of working in a life that disgusted her and hustling her butt off to please Darrell, during which she'd accomplished nothing. And for what? She'd screwed up. Darrell insinuated he'd known her identity from the beginning of their relationship. Why would he allow her to remain inside? In what way did keeping her around benefit him?

She inhaled deeply. Nothing made sense.

After everyone left and Tony and Rocki were alone, he agreed to give her space to figure things out and took Brute out for a run, despite her telling him it was a bad idea. It was dark, and Darrell's most active hours came after the sun went down. In the house, with her, would be smarter.

She was safer with Tony around, and together they'd be able to stand a chance against Darrell and his men.

Instead, he was outside by himself, no gun, practically no clothes—since he ran in shorts and sneakers only—probably bringing trouble with him. She let her head fall back against the couch. Okay, maybe he had the ability to watch out for himself.

He *was* bossy.

He had a hard body.

He picked her up and deposited her in the chair when she tried to leave without one single grunt of exertion. His chest, solid and hot against her, made her dizzy. She blew out her breath to lessen the claustrophobia of being shut inside the house and helpless. She hated to admit it, but he was right.

Tony was more than capable of protecting her. He turned from teasing to serious in a beat. She'd observed him with a weapon. He was trained, and she had no doubt highly skilled, going by the way he moved, listened, and stayed aware of what was going on. If only she felt more confident in her abilities around him. It pissed her off that deep inside, she was relying on him because her own confidence had taken a nosedive.

Tony helped keep her mom protected and out of the state—far out of the state and across an ocean. When she'd asked for help, he didn't hesitate. During the meeting with the guys from the agency, he'd stayed by her side, and she liked the attention.

In her mind, she divided her current problems into two categories: Darrell Archer and Tony Weston.

One of them she hated and feared. The other one she liked and wanted. She had neither time nor skill to handle either one.

Tony was out of her league, domineering, invincible, and tempting. Darrell...well, he just freaked her the frick out.

From everything she knew, controlling men were never happy for long, unless they were made to feel needed. At least that's what she'd gleaned from her father leaving before she even knew him. The moment a woman showed any backbone, like her mother had, they hit the door. Her father left a few months after her mom ignored his wishes and went back to work after Rocki was born.

Her mom would never admit the reason, but there were enough hints given for her to figure it out herself. Then when she became an adult, she found men intimidated by her career. They wanted a woman who couldn't outshoot, outsmart, and outstrategize them. Until now, she never felt like any of them were worth the trouble of getting them to believe in her need for a career alongside a relationship.

Two knocks followed by two more raps startled her out of her thoughts, sending her heart racing. She hurried over to the door, peeked through the eyehole, and then stepped over to the newly installed control box and shut off the alarm. She folded her arms, waiting for Tony to come in. Her stomach lurched and she swallowed her nervousness down. The stress was definitely getting to her.

How could she want him and not want him at the same time?

He swung the door open, spotted her, and his gaze turned intense. "Everything okay?"

"No." She sighed. "I don't like the idea of waiting to see what happens."

"I told—"

"I also don't like having to stay here." She paced a short path in front of him. "I don't like knowing my mom is with two strangers, probably having the time of her life, or the way everyone looks at me as if you just asked me to marry you. Have you told them our date was fake at the bar the other night?"

"No, I—"

"See! Even you aren't telling the whole truth. All I want is for someone to tell me how to take Darrell down." She untangled her arms and held her hands between them. "Look at me. I'm a mess. I'm shaking. My heart is beating all weird as if I'm going to pass out." She inhaled deeply. "I'm probably getting sick. I'm under too much stress, and staying here is not helping. I probably caught some virus from you, because you're always touching me."

God, she loved how he stuck beside her, but she was starting to depend on him to always be around. He was temporary, and despite how she was acting, he wasn't going to be here all the time to help her.

"Sweetheart," he murmured, reaching for her.

She slapped his hands away. "Stop that. I can't handle—"

"Hey…" He grabbed her wrist and pulled her toward him.

Her chest hit his, and she gasped. "You can't—"

"Shut up." He captured her mouth in a kiss.

She continued talking, and he sucked away all her words until she fell silent. Her legs wobbled, and he wrapped his arm around her, lifting her. God, he tasted good. Really good.

She stroked his tongue, kissing him deeper. He laughed against her mouth and pulled back. She frowned, licking her lips, liking the way he tasted.

His gaze warmed. "Hungry?"

"Yeah, starving," she whispered, studying him.

He held up a sack she hadn't even noticed him holding. "I stopped at the burger joint a couple miles down the road."

"You snuck French fries out of the sack," she said, rubbing her mouth.

He burst out laughing. "Right before I ran up the driveway."

She knew it. Her hunger came from the salt on his lips, not his kiss turning her into a starving lunatic. "I need to get away from you; you're distracting me."

He stuck a fry in her mouth and led her into the kitchen, carrying the rest of the food with him. She sat at the kitchen table and practically ripped the burger out of his hand.

"I should've realized you haven't eaten." He strolled to the fridge and pulled out the milk. "You'll feel better after you eat. You're probably feeling whacked out from going so long without food."

She chewed, suddenly ravished. When she finished swallowing, she answered, "Too busy to eat."

He returned to the table with two full glasses. He studied her, his mouth hard. She wiped her chin with the paper napkin and glanced away. She knew she was a sight, wolfing down the food. It was past the time to take little bites and worry about manners. She ate simply because she was starving.

"My fault," he muttered. "That won't happen again. You'll eat when you're hungry from now on."

Unsure of how to accept his semi-apology, she shrugged his concern away and remained silent. None of today's events had anything to do with him. She was the one who'd dragged him into her business. If anything, she owed him.

She wadded up the paper from her burger, her hunger appeased for the moment. "You know what bothers me the most? Gino working for Darrell."

"Don't jump to conclusions." He wiped his mouth with his hand. "I'd bet my Camaro on Darrell lying about most of the things he told you. It's how he works. He's planting doubt in your mind and buying himself time to line up all the cards. He's a player. A very skillful manipulator who's had a lifetime of practice."

Hope filled her and she leaned forward. "Then I should contact

Gino? You think he's innocent? He'll want to know what happened. We can get a team back in there and—"

"No." He dug out a few fries from the bottom of the bag and popped them into his mouth. She waited while he chewed, and then he continued, "I'm not saying Gino's clean. There was something odd about how he answered my questions about you on the phone. I understand you were undercover, but I've had a chance to work with Gino for the last several years and something didn't feel right. I want to talk to him alone without him knowing you've escaped or Darrell discovering your true identity."

"When do you plan on talking to him?" she said.

He brushed off his hands. "In the morning."

"Why can't you set something up with him tonight?"

The longer she stayed with Tony, the more complicated the case became. She needed to clear her head, toughen up, and take back control. To do that, she needed to figure out why Darrell sent her to Tony and Kage when he knew she was working undercover all along. But going against Darrell on her own was getting her nowhere. To move forward, she'd need to keep a professional distance from Tony. He messed with her mojo.

"Why don't you tell me what you're thinking?" He leaned back in the chair. "No lies this time."

"What lies?" She gazed over his shoulder at the new kitchen window.

"Where do I start?" He grinned, and she had a feeling he found her amusing. "Nails?"

"Oh." She put her hands on her lap under the table. "Yeah, that was necessary."

His mouth curved into a full smile. "Real estate?"

"What's wrong with that?" She rolled her eyes. "I could sell houses if I wanted to."

"Right." He leaned forward, captured a lock of her hair, and tugged her forward. "Sweetheart, I saw what you drive. Your Porsche does not need a timing belt, and no way could you afford a car of that caliber while working part-time painting other women's nails and selling real estate in Bay City."

Close enough to kiss him, she stared at his mouth. "Ha. I didn't lie about my car. The Porsche isn't mine. Remember, it's Darrell's car. I really do have an old Honda Accord that needs a new timing belt. It's expensive, and I haven't had time to take it into the mechanic."

"I'll fix it for you." He skimmed his lips against hers. "You can watch if you'd like."

A low pleasing sound came from her and she fought to keep from closing her eyes and wrapping herself around his body. "I'd like that."

"Me too, sweetheart." The words vibrated against her lips.

Then he was gone and she blinked. He stood beside her. Before she could ask what he was doing, he picked her up and she could only hold on to his shoulders—huge shoulders—and continue kissing him. Her hunger had nothing to do with food this time.

In the bedroom, he put her on her feet without letting go. He locked his gaze on her, smiled tenderly, and exhaled. His confidence put her at ease.

She liked how he took her choices away. Left up to her, she'd keep pushing him away, because that's what she was supposed to do, but it was also the last thing she wanted to do. "I want you to know, I don't normally sleep with men...and never on the job. I mean, I've had boyfriends, but I don't—"

He covered her mouth with his finger, sliding the tip along the width of her bottom lip. "I know."

Good. She wanted him to believe what she planned to do meant something to her. Not that she expected roses tomorrow, but she wasn't a skank. Yet she felt like one, and right now, she wanted to be the skankiest woman ever and show him she was better than all the women he'd been with before.

"I think I'm stressed," she whispered.

His chest rumbled under her hands. "Let's see what I can do to de-stress you, huh?"

She nodded, her stomach doing cartwheels as he slowly stripped her of her shirt. She quivered at the concentrated way he took in all the new discoveries he seemed to find on her body. He made her feel special and perfect, even though her hips were too slender and her breasts were too large for her frame.

He planted his mouth on her abdomen. As he tasted his way up her body, she sank her fingers into his hair, guiding him higher until he straightened in front of her.

"Your turn," she said.

He toed off his running shoes and socks. She zeroed in on the shorts hanging low on his hips. Hooking her thumbs under the waistband, she stepped closer until her nipples touched his chest and lowered the shorts.

He growled and kicked off the offending material, picked her up, and threw her on the bed, landing softly braced above her. She laughed. His reaction toward her was dangerous. He was extremely pleased.

From what she knew of Tony, he had little patience. He proved her opinion of him next. His tongue touched hers and her whole body moaned. Her legs relaxed, and his hips settled between her thighs. Heat shot through her and she melted, conforming her body to entwine with his.

Without another thought, her hands came up to his arms, over his shoulders, and around his head, holding him in position as she kissed him back. She deepened the kiss, losing herself in the security of him holding her. He controlled the situation and she let him, loved letting him lead, knowing wherever he took her would be a wonderful place she'd want to stay and enjoy herself.

"I want you," he muttered.

She lifted her hips, giving him permission. "Okay."

"Not yet." He pulled back and stared down into her eyes.

She tilted her head, languishing on the bed, barely able to question what he meant when he showed her. His head went down and he worked his way south, over her breasts, her ribs, her abdomen. She squirmed on the bed, half hoping he'd come back, enter her, and half wishing he'd continue not listening to her, because she liked where he was going.

She got her wish. His mouth sealed around her heat. She came up on her elbows, staring down at him in fascinated horror. "Uh," she panted, "Tony?"

Oh. My. God. She felt his smile against her most private spot and…and…"Never mind."

She dropped her head to the mattress and clutched the comforter. He chuckled and continuing lavishing attention on her. Who was she to argue with him over what he enjoyed doing?

The pressure, his tongue, the wildness of the night left her reaching. Tighter, higher, her insides coiled. Her heels dug into the mattress, and her whole world exploded into a bazillion little shock waves bouncing from her core out to every limb.

Softly, gently, he eased away from her letting her come down from her orgasm. She struggled to open her eyes and inhale, reconnecting with her body and becoming aware of what he was doing.

He stretched across her and opened his nightstand. She took the condom from his hand after he tore the foil. Rolling the protection on him, she caressed his hard length.

Hot, hard, perfect. Her fingers wrapped around his width, caressing him, and marveling at how his whole body impressed and intimidated her.

"That's good…" he murmured.

Her head came up and she locked her gaze on him. He barely moved, bracing himself on his elbows, yet he waited.

"Tony?" She raised her hips. "Please."

He smiled and lowered himself, teasing her pussy with his cock, until he plunged inside of her on a moan. She sucked in her breath, her throat constricting at the consuming knowledge that he filled her. It wasn't his size—though that helped—or the act of sex; it was Tony's presence. They were together, neither one winning or pressuring the other. She no longer had to keep him at a distance or worry about him making her weak. Everything she admired, his strength, focus, understanding, wrapped around her, and the relief was so great, she wanted to hold on to him and never lose the feeling he gave her.

He rocked back and forth. The friction between their bodies rubbed her sex, and she pressed against him. Her body heated, and she dug her fingers into his shoulders, accepting everything he gave.

She locked her legs around his hips. Her insides clenched, throbbing, straining. She panted, reaching for more. He buried his face in her neck and whispered, "You want it harder?"

"God, yes," she said between breaths.

He held himself above her and thrust inside of her. Pleasure sparked throughout her body, and she threw her arms out to the sides and clutched the blanket on the bed.

Tony's eyes never left her face, the absolute enjoyment in his gaze more powerful than anything he could do to her. With each plunge of his cock, her will to hold back let go, and she squirmed underneath him, giving him what he gave to her.

An upward spiral that careened out of control, she arched off the mattress and wrapped her arms around his neck as she climaxed. Tony buried himself deep inside of her, groaning his release. Exhilarated, she ran her hand up into his hair and held him against her while her body trembled.

"I knew it," he whispered.

She smiled against his shoulder. "Yeah. That was—"

Shot blasts rocked the house. His body hardened and became a wall around her. She screamed as he rolled with her across the bed and onto the floor. Settled underneath him, she shook his shoulders, wanting to get up.

"Wait," he said.

Each silent second seemed to last forever. Her heart thudded. She'd let her guard down.

Tony pushed off the floor and stood. Two more shots came. She scrambled to her hands and knees, grabbing her clothes off the floor and wiggling into them without standing. He slipped his shorts on, then his shoes, and moved around the bed to the dresser.

He took out a pistol, loaded the chamber, and passed the gun to her. Then he did the same thing again and armed himself. He looked at her. "Get my phone, hit speed dial one. Tell Lance what's going on. Then call nine one one."

She moved to follow him, but he had already turned toward the door. "Wait. We'll both go out."

"Stay put." He glanced over his shoulder. "Do not come out of the room."

Unable to process what was happening when moments ago he'd zapped her of the ability to make a conscientious decision, she simply nodded and watched him slip out of the room. Maybe having Tony take charge of the situation was a good thing.

For the last four months, she'd been on duty twenty-four seven. She let herself relax tonight, and her head wasn't in the right place.

She picked up Tony's phone. Tonight could've turned out much worse, because she'd fallen into bed and could only think about what Tony had done to her body. He'd taken her to a place where there were no bad guys or bullets aimed at her...only him.

Frick, frick, frick. She poked at the keypad on the phone. She could've been shot in the middle of an orgasm with her mouth wide-open and her fingers clutched in Tony's hair. If she'd died tonight, at least she would've died happy.

Chapter Ten

Tony returned to the bedroom fifteen minutes later after the gunfire had ceased and he'd given details on what kind of gun was fired—a forty-millimeter—and how many times—six. He paused at the door, ran his hand down his face, and shook the tension from his shoulders. A fucking drive-by. In a subdivision where families slept and children played in the street. Thank God, it was late, and everyone was inside at this time of night.

He opened the door. Rocki came off her perch at the end of the bed. "Did you see anyone?"

He shook his head, glanced over her from head to toe. She'd dressed and put her shoes on, and held the pistol in her right hand. He slipped his fingers under her arm and guided her around until her back was to the door.

"Listen, the cops are here. They're casing the outside, looking for any evidence." He lowered his voice. "My guys are here too. I think you should stay in the bedroom, away from the police."

"Why?" She frowned. "This isn't my squad. I'm in a different jurisdiction. They won't even recognize me."

Was she kidding? Every police officer in the state had taken classes at the academy. One glimpse of her, and they'd remember her for a lifetime. Hell, he'd branded her in his head the first time he saw her out in the field, teaching a weapons class.

"Because Gino got wind of what happened and he's en route." He gave her a few seconds to let the new information sink in. "I want to know how he knew something was going down at my home, and why he's taking a personal interest. I need to know if he's already found out you're in my protection."

Her shoulders went back and she glared. He narrowed his eyes back, knowing he'd predicted her reaction right. She was used to handling cases herself.

"I want to talk with Gino," she said.

He raised his gaze to the ceiling. "I had a feeling you'd say that."

"Come on, Tony. Think about it. If he's in the area, if it was Darrell or his men shooting the house, the coincidences are questionable. If Gino's dirty, I'll take him down myself."

"You'll wait in here. I'll bring you to Gino after I talk to him first. And only if I think it's safe." He dropped his hands. "Give me your word."

"Frick," she muttered. "I'm getting sick of knowing you're right."

"Rocki. My main concern is protecting you."

"Fine." She raked her teeth over her bottom lip. "I swear I'll stay in here."

"Thanks, sweetheart," he murmured, stroking her cheek with the pad of his thumb. "We're not finished. Not by a long shot."

Thinking about Gino working the underground and using the department for illegal activities killed her. She shivered. "I hate the idea."

His head went back and he dropped his hand. "Us?"

She shook her head and frowned. "What? No. I'm talking about Gino working with Darrell."

He relaxed and slipped his fingers underneath her hair at the base of her neck. "I wasn't talking about business, sweetheart. I'm not finished with what I started earlier. The bullets landing in the siding of my house stopped me from doing what I want to you and making you happy. As soon as this is over, I want you back underneath me, so I can show you how good it is between us."

Another quiver rolled through her body, remembering what he'd done to her before the shooting and the way he'd made her beg. She smiled and when he grinned in return, she seemed to gain confidence. "Really?"

He kissed her hard and fast, laughing against her lips. "Help me out, sweetheart. Don't look at me being all sweet and warm. I need to go out there, before Kage loses his patience and we have another war on our hands. He's got a personal investment in this case, whether he likes it or not, and when it comes to his uncle, Kage doesn't play around now that he has Janie."

"Oh. Okay." She fought a smile and ignored the way her mind battled with going with him or keeping him in the bedroom. She was a detective. Thoughts of having sex again with Tony had to wait. "Hurry. It drives me crazy to be shut in here while you're out doing my job. It's wrong."

"Hang tight," he said, kissing her and walking out of the bedroom.

Alone in the room, she looked down at her clothes. She'd give anything for a shower and a new outfit. Gino would see right through her and know she slept with Tony and stayed at his house in hiding.

Going to her house was out of the question, and most of her good clothes were still in Darrell's spare bedroom. She might as well count them as lost to her.

She walked into the bathroom, shut the door without making

any noise, and found Tony's brush. As she worked out the snarls in her hair, she planned what she'd say to Gino.

Tears came to her eyes. She continued brushing, blaming the emotions on the pain with every yank on the knots. She'd looked up to Gino. He was her mentor and when she was fresh out of the academy, she'd partnered with him for almost eight months until she'd entered the detective division.

She was one of the few officers who'd stayed in the same jurisdiction since graduating. With the county sheriff's office, her department, sharing the academy building, she remained in daily contact with Gino. She'd shared burgers and beer on the weekends with him and his wife on several occasions. She blinked repeatedly, dispelling the tears. Even speculating on his integrity sat wrong and she felt guilty telling Tony her suspicions.

Every man and woman in uniform deserved her support. Whether it was on duty or off, they bonded with each other under their common oath to serve and protect. The police force became family. Family never turned on one another.

Unable to resist, she returned to the bedroom and peeked out the window. She took in all the cars lining the front of the house. After fifteen minutes of watching the activity, the officers went to their cars and drove away. Kage and Lance's rides remained along with Gino's black unmarked car.

The door opened. She fisted her hands and studied Tony for any sign of what was going on outside the house.

He gave her nothing.

"Gino's waiting in the living room for you," he said, holding out his hand.

She hurried across the room toward him. Needing his strength, his reserve, she clasped his hand and received a reassured squeeze in return. "What did he say?"

"You'll find out. I don't want to muddy your opinion." He paused in the doorway. "Trust your instincts, sweetheart. This is what you do. Listen closely, and don't ignore your gut."

She nodded and let go of him.

If she wanted to run the detective division, she had to prove herself. She squared her shoulders and walked in front of him to go talk with her boss.

Gino stood beside the couch, his arms folded across his chest, his jaw set in a stony impasse. She approached him and held out her hand. "Detective Marcelli."

He shook her hand, then widened his stance and recrossed his arms. "Do you want to explain what in the hell is going on? You were to check in if anything went down with Darrell. Next thing I know, I get a call from him"—he motioned his chin toward Tony—"and all hell's breaking loose. Last time I checked, Detective, you were working under my orders."

Her body vibrated. She faced him without breaking his gaze, and took the smack down. Attitude and insubordination would get her nowhere.

"My cover with Darrell was blown after he sent me on a job to check out the men from the body shop. When I was done, Darrell waited for me. He took me back to his base, where he's been hiding in plain sight, and let me know he was privy to my identity." She looked Gino in the eye. "I escaped out of Darrell's house after he put me in lockdown, lost his guards, and broke into Weston's house to keep myself safe because I had nowhere else to go, no money, and I needed somewhere to regroup and cover myself."

"With no check-in to headquarters," Gino said.

She swallowed. "No, sir. Darrell gave me enough information to make me doubt my safety in contacting you."

Gino scowled. "What?"

"I was led to believe you're working for Darrell, or against him, as the case may be, and you have your hand in what happens in the underground," she said.

Gino stared without saying a word. Then he exploded. "Are you fucking kidding me? I trained you. Every damn thing you know came from me."

"Yes, sir," she said. "I know."

That was the reason why she stopped herself from running back. Gino trained her well, and to trust her judgment.

"Who have you mentioned this to besides Weston?" Gino remained at attention, his arms still crossed over his chest.

"We had a meeting with the other three private investigators of the body shop. Lance McCray, Garrett Beaumont, and Kage Archer." She clasped her hands behind her back, out of his direct line of vision, and clenched them together. "That's all. Tony, I mean, Weston was going to meet with you in the morning and update you on my position. I wanted to set up a meeting, but with Darrell looking for me, it would've been unwise to run straight to you. After tonight's drive-by shooting, my feeling that something wasn't right backs my decision, I believe."

Gino's muscle in his jaw twitched. "Anything else?"

"No, sir."

He unfolded his arms and approached her. Lowering his voice, he continued, "You know me, Rocki."

"Yes, sir, I do."

He nodded, glanced down at the floor. "I expect you back at the station to debrief"—he looked at his watch—"at zero seven hundred."

Tony stepped forward. "Rocki?"

She stiffened, held up her hand to Tony, and directed her attention to Gino. "Sir, I would like to take my two weeks of vacation starting today."

"You've got to be shitting me, Bangli." Gino glanced between her and Tony then nodded once. "I'll have Detective Smith watch you, until we figure out what kind of threat Darrell will be. I don't want you causing any more problems for the department. Do you understand me?"

"Yes, sir," she said.

"Save the taxpayers' money. She's staying with me, and the body shop is footing the bill," Tony said.

Gino pinned Rocki with a look she couldn't read. She held her breath. Right now if she had to choose between someone that she'd known for years, pledged her life to protect, and Tony…she'd pick Tony. He'd been right this whole time. She had to go with the vibe in the room, and something wasn't right.

"Is that what you want?" Gino waited for her to nod, and then he stretched his lips tightly over his teeth. "Fine."

"Thank you, sir." The stress of keeping alert eased and she relaxed. "Gino, I'm sorry. I did everything according to the book and relied on my smarts. I have no idea how Darrell learned my identity. I've gone over everything that happened. I kept my head and played right into his hand. There's no way he should've known."

Gino put his hand on her shoulder. "You've gone deeper than anyone and you're out, safe for now. We'll get the son of a bitch. For now, stay low, and I'll start getting you rolled back into schedule on your return. I'll discuss the options with the board. They might want you to go into the WPP, until we've got a handle on things."

The Witness Protection Program? She sucked in air. Going in, she knew that was a possibility, but until now the thought of disassociating herself with her life seemed pointless. Darrell knew everything about her. She doubted a new identity and location would stop him.

She stayed in the living room as Gino nodded at Tony and walked out the front door. She stared at the exit for several minutes, letting the last ten minutes sink in, going back through every sentence spoken.

There were too many unanswered questions. She still had no idea why Gino would show up tonight at Tony's or why he'd want her to drive in to the department in the morning when he believed she should disappear. She swallowed bile. The thought of giving up everything she worked her ass off for because of Darrell burned her throat.

Tony placed his hand on her hip. She leaned against the support. With two weeks off, she had to figure out how to get out of the mess she'd created and keep her life, her job, and those she loved and cared about safe. Her mom couldn't stay gone forever, and she had to leave Tony's house eventually.

"Are you okay?" he murmured.

"No." She moistened her lips. "Can I ask you something?"

"Yeah."

She thought over her words carefully. Once said, she couldn't take them back.

"Something isn't right." She inhaled deeply, hating the way her voice warbled. "I've noticed during past interrogations, Gino has a pattern of rubbing his thumb with his finger every time he brings up false accusations, trying to force a confession. He's aware of the problem. In fact, I was the one who brought it to his attention during training. He overcompensates for the nervous tic by crossing his arms."

"Shit," Tony said.

She looked up at him. "When he checked his watch, he was rubbing his fingers together. The rest of the time, he crossed his arms. Gino's lying and it's killing me. He's supposed to be one of the good guys. He's my mentor, and I've looked up to him for years. It kills me, because I knew better than to trust a man."

"What?" Tony frowned. "You don't trust men?"

She cut him a quick glance. "Not really."

"Then, sweetheart, we have a problem." Tony moved in front of her. "I'm going to teach you that there's one man you *can* trust. Me."

She gazed up into his eyes, so serious and intent, and knew she was in trouble. She'd let her insecurities slip out, and she had a feeling he was the one man who wouldn't run away from a challenge.

Chapter Eleven

The only thing Rocki heard in Tony's bedroom was their heavy breathing. She flung her arms out to the sides of her on the bed. Tony hovered over her.

She enjoyed the determination on his face and smiled, hoping he'd prove her wrong despite her argument that it was too soon to have sex again. "Tony, stop. I can't do it again."

He growled, nipping her neck. "Your lies seem to have no end."

"I'm serious. We've already had sex—good sex, freaking fantastic sex—twice. It's almost time to get up, and we've barely slept all night," she said, dropping her gaze to his kiss-swollen lips.

"Is that a dare?" He rolled off her and propped his elbow against the mattress, gazing into her eyes.

She curled against his chest. "Maybe…"

He inhaled swiftly before rolling back on top of her and pinning her arms above her head. He kissed her softly, slowly, and she captured his groan with her mouth. His tongue explored. The taste of him, intoxicating and addictive, electrified her.

"You keep pushing me, sweetheart, and I know exactly what you want," he breathed. "You can't lie, you can't tease, and you can't hide. Say it…you want me."

"I want you, Tony." She held his head, hoping she could give him everything he wanted. What he asked seemed simple, and she had no problem agreeing. She'd never wanted anyone more.

His quiet acceptance through the last several days attracted her. His arms comforted her. But, it was the tenderness in his touch that had her melting into him. She craved the solid dependability that Tony supplied.

She'd never found that quality with anyone else. With her father absent from her childhood, her disappointment in Gino, and all the two-dates-then-it-was-over boyfriends in her past, not once had the hole inside of her felt the comfort of knowing she was wanted more than a man's next breath. Tony put her first despite the chaos she'd thrust upon his life.

For all his gentleness, there was something raw about the way he showed her who was in control. Used to working and surviving on her own, she hadn't realized how much she wanted to depend on another person. For as long as she could remember, she'd even taken care of her mom.

Sure, Mary worked and put a roof over her head but emotionally, Rocki was the stronger one of them. Tony made it almost unbearable to think of changing his mind. A moaned emerged from her throat. There was nothing controlled about her reaction to him. She sought the comfort he could provide, the intimacy she craved.

Tony pulled back without letting her go. She wrapped herself tighter around him, not ready to move away from him.

His lips skimmed her forehead, her nose, and her lips. "Since the day I saw you at the academy over a year ago"—he laid his forehead on hers—"you've been in my head. I sleep, and there you are, tormenting me. Then I saw you with Darrell and—"

"What?" She blinked. "You said you recognized me, but—"

"Thought about you all the time. Sexiest woman I'd ever seen, you haunted me for months. Have only wanted you since. Then the day you brought Janie her cat, I was there in the parking lot. It bothered the hell out of me that you were working for Darrell," he mumbled. "You make it hard to take my time, because I've wanted you for what seems like forever and I'm not letting you go this time."

"Are you joshing me?" she whispered.

His lips caught hers, and he bit down. His blond lashes and brows stood out on an intense face with lightning-bright eyes. She squirmed. The same anticipation she was feeling showed back to her in his eyes. She caressed his cheek. He was beautiful.

He'd wanted her for a year? She had no idea.

"Rocki." He sounded hoarse. "Are you getting what I'm saying? Before, I didn't have you. I wanted you, though, but I was waiting. I wasn't going to you offer you less of a man than you deserved. Now that you're here, in my life, and I'm feeling confident that you're the woman for me, I'm ready to give you everything I've got…my time, my attention, my heart. I'm not letting you walk away from me. I want this, what we have when we're together, how I feel when you lean into me and put your hand on my stomach. Best fucking feeling in the world to know you depend on me and want that position in my life. Can't get any closer, sweetheart, than next to me all the time."

She shivered in anticipation. "I'm right here."

He cupped her head in both his hands. His fingers encompassed her cheeks. She whimpered, caught up in the way he took charge and always, no matter what she did to anger him, cherished her. His lips found hers again, the pleasure so penetrating and soulful, tears came to her eyes. She opened to him. Her body trembled with need, making it hard to keep her gaze on him. She wanted to watch what was happening between them.

He sucked in his breath, looking at her breasts. She rotated her shoulder, half hoping he approved of what he was seeing and half self-conscious he'd find her lacking. He stopped her with a kiss on the sensitive skin between her breasts.

"So beautiful…" He raised his gaze.

She smiled. "Only because of how you make me feel."

He cupped her breasts, his thumb strumming the tips until her nipples tightened into rosy beads, and then leaned across and stroked her with his tongue. She lifted, gasping, as he kissed an erect nipple, sealing his lips over the taut flesh. Rhythmic pulses arched through her body with each soft pull. She sunk her hands into his hair, holding him to her. The pleasure released a flood of emotions within her.

"Tony." She arched. "Please."

"Say my name again."

"Tony." She writhed underneath him. "I'm…Oh, oh…"

"Let me help you, sweetheart." He snatched a condom off the bed and settled between her legs.

His hardness jutted away from his body, proud and powerful, domineering like its owner. He rolled the condom on and resettled above her. His gaze held hers. His jaw clenched in determination. Her stomach fluttered. Slowly, gently, and with excruciating pleasure, she accepted his length into her wetness.

Seated deeply within her, he held himself steady. "Okay?"

"Y-yes." She locked her ankles against the small of his back.

After a moment, he moved. "Mine, sweetheart. This is all mine."

He eased back in tormenting slowness. Then plunged with determination, making her gasp. He shifted, leaning on his elbows and cradling her head in his hands. "Look at me."

"Yes."

He quickened his pace.

She tentatively arched up to meet each thrust, becoming bolder as her body accepted his size. He shifted, and her body recovered from its earlier release. She grasped his face in her hands.

"Come for me," he whispered.

His deep voice rolled over her. She exploded, squeezing him as she poignantly quivered. He grunted, holding himself still above her.

"We have something special. You feel it?" he growled.

She panted, trying to slow her racing heart. Her chest beat against his. *God, I can't even think.*

"Say it," he squeezed out between clenched teeth.

"Yeah." She kissed his cheeks, his lips, and his chin. "I feel it."

He visibly relaxed, before he eased out of her. She must've voiced her displeasure over the loss of his body, because he turned and smiled one of those killer smiles that reached his eyes and showed how much she pleased him. "I'll be right back."

He strolled naked into the bathroom. She fought to keep her eyelids open and failed. Never had a man made her believe what they shared was so special, she found herself wishing for the impossible. Tony left her saturated. She couldn't come up with a good reason not to believe they had something real in such a short time.

The next thing she knew, Tony pulled her across the length of the bed. She struggled awake, clutching at his arms. "Wh-what time is it?"

"Two in the afternoon. You slept the morning away." He kissed her hard. "Shower, get dressed, we gotta go out of the house."

"Where?" She stumbled out of bed and rubbed the hair out of her eyes.

"It's a surprise and you'll be safe." He raised his brows and grinned. "Fifteen minutes. Hurry."

She walked, wobbly, to the bathroom. Tony cleared his throat, and she glanced over her shoulder. "What?"

"Sweetheart," he murmured, his mouth softening as his gaze went down to her lower body. "Are you sore?"

Warmth rushed to the surface of her chest and face. She wasn't sore. She was perfect. "No. Loose."

"Loose?" His eyes crinkled at the corner.

She grinned. "It's a good thing, Weston. Trust me."

His shoulders rounded and he laughed. She stood, naked and un-embarrassed, and completely in lust with the man in front of her. He was gorgeous, but when he laughed, he was irresistible. She walked straight toward him. Loose hipped and tingling in places she normally paid no attention to, Rocki wrapped her arms around him.

He swept her up and nuzzled her neck. "Damn, you're hilarious."

She framed his face with her hands. "No joking, Weston. I'm in danger of losing my heart with you if I'm not careful."

He set her on her feet slowly. "If you don't, I'll be pissed. You're mine."

She laughed and when he flinched, she stopped. "Are you serious?"

"How could you think otherwise," he said.

"We...Sex..." She fluttered her hand. "I thought you were saying those things because you wanted me for sex."

He shook his head. She bit down on her lower lip. *Shit.*

He leaned toward her, kissed her gently, and whispered. "Keep feeling it. Listen, touch, taste—it's all there. I've had a year to think of nothing else."

Then he walked out of the room. She stared at the empty doorway. Tough-guy Weston was serious. She harrumphed right before she smiled and hurried into the bathroom.

Chapter Twelve

Outside the city limits of Bay City, on a rural road on the west side of town, Tony parked the car in front of a single-story ranch house in need of a paint job, but the flowers planted in front of the big window brightened the older house. She climbed out of the car and met Tony at the front bumper.

"Whose house is this?" she asked.

"Kage lives here." Tony slipped his fingers into her hand. "He likes the solitude."

The area fit Kage, who she assumed was a loner because the only time he put any effort into talking was when Janie was with him. She imagined any man as quiet and serious as him appreciated time to himself.

Tony lifted her hand and kissed her knuckles as he walked her up onto the porch. "You're walking funny again."

"Shut up," she hissed out. "The *funny* has nothing to do with you. For your information, the idea of wearing the same pair of panties for three days ended two days ago, so I'm going commando under the shorts. It's not like you've left me alone long enough for me to put them in the washing machine."

He stopped. "No shit? You're naked under the shorts?"

"Come on, Weston." She tugged on his hand, keeping a firm grip with her other hand on the waistband of Tony's shorts, which she happened to be wearing because she refused to put on her dirty outfit that she escaped Darrell's house in. "It was your idea to come to Kage's. Let's get it over with...and don't say a word about my lack of clothing. It's bad enough I have to wear your Harley T-shirt out in public with your gym shorts. At least we don't have to worry about Darrell or one of his thugs recognizing me out in public. I look like a freak."

His gaze grew heated. "I told you what would happen if you continued calling me by my last name. I don't get why you can't call me Tony. We're having sex. I'm not Weston to you. The guys in there, sure, but not you."

She rolled her eyes. He'd stripped her of his jersey last night, because she refused to call him Tony, and proceeded to prove to her what she'd get if she didn't stop using his last name. Not that she minded his lesson. The guy was good with his hands, she'd give him that much. Must be from polishing all the chrome he had on his Camaro.

"You're pathetic." She didn't understand what the big deal was over calling him by his last name.

"Then explain why you keep saying Weston," he said.

She folded her arms and tapped her foot. "Because it's sexy."

"Try again."

She tossed her ponytail behind her shoulder. "So I won't forget your last name."

"Liar."

"You have a hard time trusting me. Have you ever thought you might need a therapist for your unwillingness to have faith in others?" She turned around marched to the door and knocked. "Let's get this show on the road, and do whatever we came here to do instead of arguing about names."

Tony slipped in front of her and opened the door, not waiting for Kage to answer. She snorted and followed him inside, wanting to be anywhere but with the guys. Like maybe hanging out at Tony's house doing her laundry to wash her freaking panties.

"Yo," Lance called from further inside the house. "We're in the kitchen. Girls are sequestered in the bedroom. I'd warn you not to go in there. It's not safe for any male."

Tony changed directions and pushed her down a hallway. She braced her feet, but she was no match for his strength.

"What are you doing?" she said, scrambling to keep from falling.

He stopped, kissed her, and pushed her inside a room before slamming the door. She grasped the handle as laughter came from behind her. She turned and sagged against the door.

She wasn't alone.

Janie stood in front of the bed, pursing her lips, stiff, and prepared for anything. Rocki slid her gaze to another woman standing at the closet door. Whoa, talk about a fashionista. The blonde-haired woman's clothes had come right off the model.

Both women studied her intently, and she pressed her back against the door.

"Uh, hi." She waved with one hand, reached for the door handle with the other hand, and lost Tony's shorts in the process. Heat flooded her face, and she bent at the waist to pull the shorts back up.

Janie snorted, while approaching her. "Kick them off. We're here to make sure you're dressed like a girl. Trust me"—she pointed at the other woman in the room—"Sabrina has enough clothes to share. She's my best friend and cool, so treat her right or you deal with me."

Rocki stiffened. "I'm not here to hurt anyone."

"I know that now, but the other day, I would've kicked your ass if

Kage hadn't been there." Janie shrugged. "We'll talk more later. We need to get you dressed like a woman. Instead of a…whatever it is Tony has you wearing."

She tugged at the hem of her shirt, making sure they couldn't see her bare ass. "I'm going to kill Weston," she mumbled.

"Are you doped?" Sabrina said. "Why would you want to harm a hair on Tony's sexy body?"

She stared at the gorgeous woman. Platinum-blonde hair cut short and chic framed an almost pixie-like face with the most impish grin she'd ever seen. Not to mention the torn jean shorts, jean vest sans shirt that showed off a lot of skin, and red high heels that made Rocki feel like the ugly tomboy of the group in Tony's clothes. She glanced behind her at the shorts on the floor. Well, she still wore his shirt.

Janie, of course, looked sexy and relaxed in a short sundress, deep tan, and bare feet. What was Tony doing, bringing her here to these two women? Kage's girlfriend hated her and she had no idea who Sabrina was or if she should be worried.

"Um, it's a long story. But if I told you I'm standing here with no panties on talking to a woman who'd rather hurt me and one I think walked out of the center of a magazine, in a house I've never been to before, and the man I'm sleeping with believes we're in a committed relationship after only knowing each other four days and seems to think it's a crime if I call him by his last name"—she inhaled deeply and shrugged—"then the answer is yes. I must be doped."

Sabrina and Janie stared at her with their mouths open. She backed away. The girls looked at each other, cracked up, and lunged toward her. Unable to do anything but allow them to pull her forward and plop her down on the edge of the bed, she prayed she'd die…right on the spot.

"Tony called you his woman?" Sabrina clasped her hands in front of her and seemed to have an urge to pee. "Spill, and don't leave out any details, no matter how insignificant. We'll need every single one."

"Yeah, he called me his woman," she mumbled. "He's a serious guy, I guess."

"God, this is good." Janie bounced on the mattress. "I knew it. When he interrogated Kage about you after you showed up with his uncle a couple of months ago at Corner Pocket, I knew he was crushing on you big-time."

Crushing? She frowned. "What did he say?"

Janie waved her hand in the air, dismissing the question. "I take it you're not working for Kage's uncle. Tony would be all up in Darrell's shit if you were."

She shook her head. "No, I'm a detective. I was working undercover—"

"That's brilliant." Janie jumped to her feet, pulled Sabrina off the bed, and pushed her toward the bags. "Get the clothes for Rocki."

"Honestly, I don't need any…" She worried her lip, having second thoughts. "You wouldn't happen to have any new panties in one of those bags, would you?"

Sabrina cast a glance at her she didn't understand, rifled through the sacks, and tossed her one, two, three pairs of panties with price tags still on them. She caught them all, tearing off a tag, and slipped the red pair on. More comfortable covered, she relaxed for the first time since stepping inside Kage's house. "I promise to give everything back when I'm done with the case."

"Please don't." Sabrina's brows rose and she leaned backward without looking at what she was pulling out of the bags. "I'm a shopaholic. If I share the clothes or give them away, it means I get to buy more. You're doing me a favor."

Janie nodded. "It's true. Sab lives for this kind of thing. Most of the clothes in my closet came out of Sabrina's closet. She'll be your new clothes supplier."

"How do you afford your habit?" Rocki stood and slipped on a pair of jeans.

Sabrina carried a few more articles of clothing over. "My dad's a senator. Let's just say he wants me to stay out of trouble and happy. I've learned it's no use arguing about him spoiling me, because he'll find another way to involve himself in my life. Personally, I think he's scared I'll bring scandal down on the family, and he's up for re-election next year. It's a sensitive time, politically."

"Senator Wilcox?" she said.

"The one and only." Sabrina sighed. "Try on this top with this jean skirt. I have a shirt exactly like it in lavender."

She gaped. "There's a difference? It looks purple to me."

"Girl, major difference in color. One's winter, one's spring." Sabrina turned back to the mess of clothes on the floor. "What size shoes do you wear?"

"Eight."

Sabrina looked at Janie. "Mine are out."

"I'll go through my closet. I wear a seven and a half shoe." Janie hurried over to the walk-in closet. "I'm sure there's something that'll be comfortable enough to wear."

Who were these women? Any girlfriend she'd had in the past dropped to the wayside when she enrolled in the academy. If she had free time in her busy schedule, she spent a couple hours with a few of the men on the force having a beer or hanging out with her mom. From what she knew, women did not hand a stranger clothes—going by the looks of the outfits, they were name-brand and classy. Not to mention sexy as all get out, and she couldn't wait to have Tony see her in them.

Standing in front of the mirror, she admired a cute, sheer shirt that hung off one shoulder and a jean miniskirt with studs lining the pockets. She caught Janie's gaze in the reflection and swallowed hard. Janie studied her but instead of looking away, she smiled. Rocki returned her smile.

For the few seconds they connected, she understood what Janie wasn't saying. Kage's girlfriend held no hard feelings for how they'd met. Whether that was part of Tony's doing or Janie had decided Rocki's being a detective meant she wasn't on Janie's boyfriend's uncle's side, she couldn't guess.

She turned and searched the room, found the cat she'd helped keep safe when Darrell kidnapped the kitty a couple months ago. She looked toward Janie to apologize for her part in keeping her cat away from her, but Janie shook her head.

"Can I hold her?" Rocki whispered.

Janie scooped the sleeping cat off the bed and handed her to Rocki. "Her name's Bluff."

"I remember," she whispered.

Rocki cuddled Bluff to her chest and stroked her soft fur. More than one good thing came of having her life in danger and flipped upside down. She would've never met Tony or Janie or Sabrina, Kage, Lance, Garrett. She sighed and gave Bluff one more squeeze before putting her on the pillow.

"I'll pay you both back for the clothes." She smoothed the material of the skirt. "The moment I can convince Weston to swing by an ATM machine and let me withdraw some money, I'll have Tony bring you the cash."

"Don't worry about it." Sabrina grinned. "When the drama you're involved in is over, I'll call and we'll do the outlets. If I see something I can't live without, I'll let you buy it."

She smiled, because those were plans she looked forward to and, not knowing what would happen in the future, she hoped Sabrina was telling her the truth. "Deal."

Sabrina walked across the room, peeked out into the hallway, and reclosed the door quietly. "Now that Rocki's settled, I need girl help from both of you."

"Name it." Janie sat on the bed and pulled Rocki down beside her.

"Kage doesn't have a case he's working on tonight, does he?" Sabrina asked.

"No. He came off one early this morning. Unless something comes up and he's called away, he doesn't have any agency work until Tuesday." Janie spun the bracelet on her arm. "Why?"

"Good. Since Tony's off duty while he sexes Rocki, I need to have a night out with the girls. Garrett's driving me crazy, and I've decided I need a new plan of action. I want to run it past you both and get your opinion." Sabrina stuck out her bottom lip and blew her bangs off her forehead.

"Wait a minute. Tony's not…sexing me," she said.

The idea of staying with Tony for the sole purpose of hooking up with him, well, that was not the reason she was with him. She had a drug lord aiming to kill her and anyone who got in his way. Although Tony had said she was his. Whatever that meant. He wasn't *just* sexing her.

Janie nudged her shoulder. "You're in his bed. He sexes you. Trust me. Kage is the same way."

She had a point. They were having a lot of sex. She wrinkled her nose. "I really need to talk to him and straighten our relationship out."

Sabrina shook her finger. "Later. This is my time, babes."

"You see, she gets grouchy when it comes to my brother. She's been hot for him for four years, even though she kept it a secret from me," Janie whispered. "Everyone knows how she feels about Garrett, except Garrett. She's pretty out-there with her attempts at flirting. He's clueless."

"Ah." She nodded, even though she didn't understand. "What can I do?"

Sabrina grinned. "I'm glad you asked."

"Uh-oh," Janie mumbled. "I thought we'd have twenty-four hours without any excitement. The last time I manipulated the boys into doing what we wanted, Kage locked me in the bedroom for two days."

She whirled to look at Janie. "What?"

"Oh, don't worry. He was locked inside with me." Janie's shoulders rounded and her eyes grew lazy. "Actually, it was nice. More than nice; it was spectacular."

Rocki glanced between the two women. A bad feeling crept in. Then she thought about all the ways they'd helped her today. She stood, willing to assist Sabrina in return for giving her clothes to wear. Besides, it felt freaking fantastic to be wearing panties again.

Chapter Thirteen

In the kitchen, while the girls kept busy doing whatever girls did when alone, Tony stared down Kage. He wanted to punch someone. There were lines Kage shouldn't cross because he was an Archer, and because of his deep responsibilities he was willing to step foot in the wrong direction to help Tony. Tony gritted his teeth. He knew damn well if Kage went in that direction, he'd regret it.

Tony slapped the table in frustration. "You gave me your word. We decided to wait."

"She's your woman," Kage said, unfazed. "Tell me she doesn't mean shit to you, and we won't go."

Tony gritted his teeth. Rocki's safety came first, but the cost of Kage putting himself in the direct path of his uncle sat wrong. He glanced at Garrett. Although they were all friends, Garrett made the final decision. He knew the rules. Their women came first over all laws and PI business.

"She calls me Weston," he murmured. "Half the time she's right there with me, feeling the same thing I am. The next, she's all in my face, pushing me away, and refusing to call me by my name."

"She's scared, bro." Kage's voice dropped. "That's why we need to go to the Crystal Palace. Trust me. Uncle Darrell will eat you alive if you take a defensive approach."

"Not that I don't respect you for staying away from him, but Rocki worked for him. It's personal with her too. Darrell's not going to let her return to the force and trust her to keep her lips shut. I've known her four days. The girl can't stay quiet. She's got a temper and lets loose before she thinks." Tony scraped his chair back and stood.

Kage sat forward. "He respects my position in the family."

Tony sucked in his breath. Kage had never claimed a connection with Darrell or divulged how he'd made their relationship—or nonrelationship—work this long. He'd spent a lifetime ignoring Darrell to Tony's frustration. He whistled, recognizing his game plan.

"You stayed in plain sight, where he could keep tabs on you," he said. "That's how you've stayed clear all this time."

Kage dipped his chin. "So, are we going to the Palace?"

Tony looked at Garrett, received a voluntary nod he was in on the deal. Tony rolled his shoulders in defeat. He was outnumbered. "I'm in, but the girls stay home."

Kage's face softened. "Right."

"I'm serious. You can't let Janie talk you into going with us. If Rocki finds out you've given your girlfriend permission to go with us, I'll never be able to keep Rocki away. She'll pull the badge, and use that power over me." Tony scowled.

"Hell, you two are pussy-whipped." Garrett laughed. "You'll never see any woman lead me around by my dick."

Feminine giggles reached the kitchen. Tony stepped back from the table and leaned against the counter, his gaze on the entrance when Rocki led the other girls into the room. His chest tightened and the air escaped his lungs.

Knockout gorgeous in a skimpy skirt, all legs, and a purple shirt hugging her breasts, Rocki surpassed any fantasy he'd created in his head. He moved in front of her and whispered, "Damn, sweetheart."

She leaned into him, hiding a smile he could still see in her eyes. "Thanks for asking Janie and Sabrina to help me. It feels good to have clothes on that fit."

He raised her chin, kissed her, and took another ogle at her legs. "Damn."

She threw her arms around his waist, buried her head into his neck, and hugged him. He stiffened, taken by surprise. He'd received hugs from his mom, Janie, and even Sabrina when her emotions overcame her—which was almost weekly—but not from Rocki. He held her against him. She always went from cold to hot, and then they got crazy. Damned if he didn't like standing here doing nothing but hugging her back.

"No fucking way," Kage said, his voice deepening.

Tony's head came up and before he could take in the situation, Rocki pulled him down for a kiss. He pressed his hand against her lower back, pulling her closer. Yeah, he liked these hugs.

She kissed him softly again before pulling away. "Wes—Tony?"

He growled. "Like that, sweetheart."

"I'm glad." She smiled, and he was blasted by how hot she looked standing this close, staring up into his eyes. "Do you mind if I take a couple of hours and hang out with Janie and Sabrina?"

He extracted himself from her, wondering if she'd overheard their plan. "Yeah, that's fine. The guys and I are running to the Crystal Palace to check things out, and I like the idea you're here, safe. I'll come and pick you up when I'm done."

"Let me go too." She leaned forward and whispered, "Darrell will be there, and I don't want you going it alone. Besides, I've been thinking about how we're going about handling Darrell, and we're wrong. We're hoping he comes after me, and he won't. He likes to do things at night, alone, without any witnesses. You live in a subdivision where someone is always around."

"Then explain the bullet holes in my siding to me," he said.

She planted her hands on his stomach. "It's his men, not Darrell. We need to go into his territory and push him. I've been to the Crystal Palace with him many times. I know he stays in the rooms downstairs with the cameras. People come to him. He never goes out on the floor, ever. We'll go and play a few slots, work the room, and flaunt how we're not scared of him. Kage and Janie can come. So can Sabrina and Garrett. Come on, even civilians know there's safety in numbers. There are six of us. We'll be safe."

"You should be scared of him." He looked toward Garrett. "Back me up, man."

Garrett pulled out a chair, set his booted foot on the seat, and braced his elbow on his knee. "Not on your life. I keep telling you, women only turn you into a pussy. You got yourself into this mess. I'm not helping you figure a way out."

In the end, Kage motioned for him to let Rocki stay with the girls. Tony held Rocki's arms and planted her in a chair at the kitchen table. She'd have company while she waited for him to come home.

"We'll talk later. Why don't you try to clear your head tonight, and tomorrow, I'll listen to one of your other plans. While I find out more information Janie and Sabrina will entertain you. Paint each other's nails... You're good at that." He grinned at his cleverness. "Sell them some real estate."

"Not laughing, Weston." Rocki folded her arms. "I'm a detective. This is my case."

He squatted beside her chair. "I know you are, and a damn good one. Do this one thing for me. Tomorrow, you're back on the case

and we go at it together. The Palace…I don't want my woman there.
At all."

Her gaze warmed. "I want to go," she whispered.

"I know, but I'm asking you to stay here and let me check things
out first." He tilted his chin, looked down at her legs, and mumbled.
"You're mine. I don't want anyone else seeing you all pretty with
your legs showing, especially Darrell. Can you give me that much?"

Janie walked away from Kage and stood by Rocki. "It's okay. We'll
stay with her."

"I think this is ridiculous. I go after suspects all the time. I *lived*
with Darrell," Rocki said.

He stood, not enjoying the reminder of where she'd resided and
what had happened during her four months with the drug lord. He
laid his hand on her shoulder. Her neck arched and she gazed at
him. "Fine. I'll stay."

Leaning down, he kissed her. "I'll make it up to you later."

"Uh, yeah, you will." She sighed and muttered, "Stupid man."

A half hour later, Tony left with the other guys, making sure they
locked up and set the security alarm. Each of them took their own
vehicle and headed to the body shop. There, they showered and
changed into clothes they'd left at the garage for agency work. Kage
pulled enough cash out of the agency's emergency drawer to give
them a few hours of playing time at the tables, and handed it over
to everyone else. Tony eyed Kage for a beat, and received a shrug in
return. Kage never gambled. Activities that bordered on illegal went
against how he chose to live his life.

Tony headed to the showers. Within three minutes, he was out,
shaking his head, preferring the uncombed look. He donned a buttoned long-sleeved shirt, black jeans, and black biker boots. He
carried the sport coat out of the bathroom and, not for the first time,
thought about redoing his bathroom at home.

The restroom Garrett put in when he built the addition for the agency behind the body shop was sweet. Tile everywhere, towel warmers, more shower heads than a person possibly needed, and automatic flushers, water, and soap dispensers. Best of all, the floor was heated and the wall-length mirror never fogged.

Kage stuck his head inside the room. "Ready to roll?"

"Yeah." He swung his coat over his shoulder and followed Kage out of the building.

The plan was clear. He headed toward his own car, having no reason to talk about what would happen when they walked into the Palace. They were a team. They worked and played together all their lives. They knew what they were going for and they'd get the job done.

He pulled out of the parking lot, following Kage. Garrett trailed him, and Lance brought up the rear of their caravan. Yeah, people would notice their arrival. They had the best vehicles in Bay City.

In the perfect scenario, he'd end the business with Darrell tonight. Put a scare in him, make him fuck up, and slam his ass in prison. He wanted him behind bars for messing with his woman, and for the shit he'd put Kage through his whole life. A few weeks or forever in prison, it didn't matter. All he needed was time without Darrell breathing down Rocki's neck and threatening what was important to Tony.

Five minutes later, he pulled into the covered entrance to the Crystal Palace, rolled down his window, and after slipping the valet twenty dollars—because nobody, not his friends or family, sat their ass in the driver's seat of his Camaro—he parked his own car.

Before he left the vehicle, he undid the snap on his holster strapped to his ribs and slid into his jacket. No one would guess he was carrying, unless a trained eye was in the room. If security questioned him, he had a concealed weapons permit in his wallet.

He spotted Kage and Garrett exiting their vehicles at the same time Lance rolled in on his Harley-Davidson. As a team, they all converged in front of the doors to the casino.

"Since this is business and I'm not using my money, I'm gonna have some fun," Lance said, stepping forward and setting the electric doors to slide open.

"It's coming out of your paycheck, asshole." Kage gazed straight ahead, but the slight twinge at his jaw took the sting out of his words.

"Keep your head up and ears open." Garrett strolled in, looking around. "Stay in sight. Don't spend more than two minutes at any table. We want to fit in and buy us some time."

Tony sauntered off on his own, checking the placement of the cameras. More protected than a military base, the Crystal Palace put him on edge. He eased the tension in his shoulders, hooked his left hand in his front pocket, and forced himself to relax and look natural. Inside, he wanted to storm the back offices and make his way down to the hidden rooms below. He wanted blood. Nobody fucked with Rocki.

Chapter Fourteen

Across the street from the Crystal Palace, sitting in Janie's souped-up red Duster with the freaky shifter, which Janie called a bitch slap, Rocki shook her head in disbelief. Whatever kind of gearshift Kage had installed in the vehicle for Janie, it was the shiggles. She wanted one installed on her Honda if she got out of this alive.

"Pull over here, we need to talk." Rocki gazed up at the polished casino building, with its flashing white lights and board announcing tonight's entertainment—Eddie and the Bangers.

"What's the deal?" Sabrina leaned forward and stuck her head between the driver and passenger seat. "If we don't hurry, the boys will leave and we won't be able to share a drink. I need to see Garrett. He's inside and that means tonight might be the night he notices I'm alive."

Janie parked along the curb and left the car to idle. Rocki swiveled in her seat to face Sabrina in the back. They should never have left the house, and if she had known Sabrina and Janie were headed to the Crystal Palace instead of Corner Pocket for a drink, she would've argued for them to stay home.

Now she regretted her rash decision. The other girls had no idea what kind of danger they'd get into coming to the casino despite the fact that this was exactly where Rocki wanted to be. The best plan she had was to meet Darrell in a public place, where it would be safe. She'd wanted to discuss her decision with Tony before he'd rushed out of Kage's house, but he was determined not to listen.

"Change of plans." She pointed her finger at both of them. "You'll drop me off, alone. Go home and sit by your phone. I'm going inside to talk to Tony."

Janie gaped at her. "Are you serious? What's the big deal where we go out to have a drink?"

"Girl, this is my night. I asked you to come along." Sabrina finger-combed her bangs. "Garrett is my man. Where he goes, I go. You said you'd go out with us."

"I know, and soon I'll help you get Garrett's attention. But, tonight is not that night, not with me with you. I have men out to kill me. I don't want you to get in trouble," she said. "The boys'll be angry when they see you with me. Besides, the odds are high that Darrell Archer is inside the Crystal Palace. He'd like nothing more than to take me out of the picture. It's not safe for us to go inside."

"You don't get it." Sabrina pressed her hand to her stomach and heaved a sigh. "You might know Tony, but you don't know Tony, Lance, Kage, and Garrett when they're together. No one messes with them. Not even Darrell."

Janie pulled on her seat belt and half turned in the driver's seat. "The thing is, Rocki, you're with one of the guys, and that makes you one of us. We understand you. We like you. We're going together or not at all. That's how we do things. Your choice. We can call tonight off and wait until your case is closed to go out for drinks. It was a bad idea to come here, but we've all been here before. Darrell never makes a move inside his own establishments."

Dammit. She looked away and blinked hard. She worked with all men, and not one of them was here helping her. Two women she barely knew were willing to have her back. What was she supposed to do?

Tonight was a perfect opportunity to meet with Darrell and be able to walk away without getting killed. There was no way he could remove her from the casino with the Beaumont Body Shop guys around. Though when Tony found out she'd gone behind his back, there would be hell to pay.

"I'm the only one packing protection, and I'm trained to defend myself. I'm good, but I can't be accountable for you two while we're inside, and this is the perfect opportunity for me to meet with Darrell while he knows I'm not alone." She unclipped her seat belt. Someone had to be the responsible one of the group and lay down the facts.

"No problem. I've got myself covered." Janie reached into her purse between the seats. "I have Mace. Sure, it's not as cool as having a gun, but Kage has something against me carrying a loaded weapon. He can be a dumbass about certain things, and apparently pistols or stealing a weapon with bullets is a trigger point with him."

Together, she and Jane looked at Sabrina. They'd have to figure out what to do with the fashionista of the group.

"Hey!" Sabrina grabbed her big black leather tote. "You two aren't the only ones who protect yourselves when you go out on the town."

Out came a leather bullwhip. At least six feet long, black, and wicked cool looking. Rocki stared in fascinated horror.

"What the hell is that?" Janie's mouth opened and she grabbed the end of the whip. "That's real leather, girl."

"Well, duh. I wouldn't buy faux leather." Sabrina coiled her weapon into a neat round circle. "I bought it for Garrett last week, and he refused to accept it." She looked at Janie. "Your brother, in typical testosterone style, thought I was propositioning him. Of course, I was…but the things that man said he was going to do to me had my panties—"

"No." Janie covered her ears. "This is my *brother* you're talking about. I don't want to know what goes on between you two."

"Okay, enough." Rocki inhaled deeply. "We'll walk inside, and I want you two to stay together. Go directly to the guys, and tell them I'm downstairs but don't let them rush to me. I need five minutes alone with Darrel. You two will remain safe, and I'll go ahead with my plan."

The two girls nodded. Rocki pushed past her doubts and lifted her chin. "All right."

Now that Rocki trusted they were all on the same game plan together, and had some way to protect themselves once they reached the inside of the casino. They'd find the boys, and she'd work her way to the bottom floor of the Crystal Palace. Both girls were brave and smart enough to draw attention to them if they found themselves in trouble. The Crystal Palace was a public place, and the bigger the group, the safer. With luck, she could catch the drug lord off guard, get the information she needed, and get out of there without any trouble.

She'd worry about the retaliation from Darrell later. It couldn't get any worse. He'd already tried to shoot her.

She turned back around and faced the front of the car. "Okay, we'll go inside. Make sure you stay close to me."

Three women dressed in the highest fashion, their hair sprayed out to freaking there, and willing to risk life or fingernail, would scare any man. She steeled her shoulders. Hopefully, Darrell and his thugs wouldn't recognize them the moment they strolled through the doors. She'd led him to believe she was malleable, obedient, and oblivious while she worked with him.

"Okay. We're ready." Rocki buckled her seat belt. "Go ahead and pull into the parking lot."

Janie drove, while Rocki filled them in on the rest of the plan. The other girls' positivity and excitement fueled Rocki. As long as she kept her head and stayed aware of what was going on around her, they'd be okay.

After stopping in front of the valet, she exited the car, hooked her arms through Janie and Sabrina's elbows as the valet drove away in the Duster, confident the men inside the casino wouldn't know what hit them when they went inside.

"Let's do this, girls," she said. "You'll go straight to the boys and make them aware of the situation. I need five minutes after I reach the elevators."

With Janie's advice that the boys would never get caught playing slots, they headed through the machines to the back lounge. Rocki scoped the area, spotted the security man who watched over the back hallway, and pulled the girls over to the side of the room.

"Do me a favor." She turned her back to the hallway. "I need you both to cause a scene and draw out the man in the black suit with the long sideburns." She pulled Sabrina back in front of her. "Don't look. As soon as I'm out of sight, go to Tony. Got it?"

They both nodded, and Janie said, "Be careful. I hate Darrell and even though I don't think he'll do anything tonight, he'll come after you another time."

"I'll be fine." She pushed them away. "Hurry."

Rocki wandered off in the opposite direction, found a spot near the hallway, but kept her attention off the man. A wild shriek followed by a feminine argument had her looking over her shoulder.

Janie stood in her heels, toe to toe with Sabrina, and called her a bitch. Sabrina shoved Janie, throwing in her own insults. Rocki clamped her teeth together to keep from smiling. If she didn't know better, it appeared as if a major girl fight was going down.

The security man walked toward the arguing girls. Rocki pivoted and slipped into the hallway. Not wasting any time, she jogged toward the elevator. Three seconds later, she was inside and heading down. She removed the pistol from her purse.

There would be guards the moment the doors opened. She flipped off the safety on the pistol and raised her gun hand. The elevator dinged and came to a lurching stop. Rocki's stomach somersaulted as the doors opened. Her stomach dropped.

Frick.

Darrell, backed by his four thugs, stood in the hallway with pistols raised. She slipped her gun back into her purse, lifted a shoulder in an attempt to act as if she'd mistakenly taken the wrong elevator, and did what was starting to become a habit and said, "Hey."

Darrell's dark eyes grew even darker and his mouth hardened. "Follow me, please."

Chapter Fifteen

One minute, Rocki, Janie, and Sabrina were standing in the hallway with the security guard, and the next Tony had lost Rocki and two more men appeared, blocking his view of the hallway. Tony threw an uppercut to the thug taking a swing at Kage. The burn on his knuckles never came, because the one person he focused on had disappeared into the elevators.

A blond man rebounded and lashed out, tearing Tony's shirt at the shoulder. Tony glanced down. *Son of a bitch.*

He fisted his hand and popped the guy square in the nose. The man hit the floor with a solid *thunk*. Tony swung his attention to Kage and found him toying with the man who'd put his hands on Janie to tear her away from Sabrina.

"Put him down," he said. "Take the girls and wait in the lounge. I'm going downstairs."

Kage shrugged, brought back his arm, and threw an uppercut that sucked the air right out of the man, and he landed beside his buddy.

Two down. What a joke. It wasn't even a fair fight.

Garrett stood against the wall, his arms folded across his chest, appearing as if he was watching a Friday night fight at the gym. "Doors open and room's empty."

Tony cussed under his breath. Damn Rocki. She forced him to take care of cleaning up her business, and he'd wasted valuable time.

"Let's drag these assholes in the room, and then get out of here." He picked up both feet of his victim and dragged him into the empty conference room off the hallway.

The whole fight took less than three minutes. The pretty boys postured and preened, but obviously had no street smarts when dealing with men who worked with their hands every day.

Once they were done hiding the unconscious bodies, buying them time until they snapped out and either hightailed it out of the casino or sought out Darrell, Tony jogged to the elevator leaving Kage and Garrett to watch Janie and Sabrina. Tony had gone below the casino a few times during investigations, but Darrell always received word ahead of time and stayed out of sight. At least he knew the layout of the floor, and it would make finding Rocki that much easier.

The elevator doors opened. Tony stuck his head out, checked the area, moved directly to the far wall, and looked in both directions. One woman in a sealed-off area, and the place appeared deserted. Not a good sign.

In practiced, controlled actions he moved down the hallway silently. He counted the cameras. One, two, three. At the end of the floor, he stepped to the side, took a second to make sure no one was coming, and kicked in the door.

Tony held his pistol in front of him and scanned the room.

Rocki paced in front of the window, her gun hand lax at her side. Darrell stood at his desk, five paces away from her. He aimed the pistol at Darrell, walking within three feet of the drug lord, the bead of his shot solid on Darrell's forehead.

"Rocki?" he said, not taking his eyes off Darrell.

Rocki scoffed. "Put your pistol down, Weston."

What the fuck? He shifted to the left, moving closer to Rocki without losing Darrell in his vision or putting down his weapon. "Explain."

She pointed to Darrell. "Let him tell you."

"She knows what's on the table." Darrell hitched his hip against the desk, and left one foot on the floor.

Rocki stepped beside him and crossed her arms. "You started it. You can finish it by telling Weston yourself."

Darrell smirked. "That's debatable. You barged into the casino."

"Because I knew you were here and I'm not going to sit around waiting for you to catch me by surprise," Rocki said.

"Were you not listening?" Darrell's brow twitched.

Rocki huffed. "I heard, but did you hear?"

This was not happening.

"Both of you shut up." He stepped closer to Darrell. "You first."

Darrell titled his chin and beyond Tony to the open doorway. "I see my nephew left you alone."

"Since you've had cameras on us the whole time, you know exactly what Kage is doing. You also know we took out three of your men, so I have to ask myself why you'd stay below if you knew trouble was headed in your direction." Tony stood blocking Darrell's view of Rocki. "But first, I want to know what the fuck you're doing in the same room as my girl."

"Put the weapon away, and I'll talk to you." Darrell held up his hands. "I'm alone. Your woman is safe. There's no reason we can't get along."

Tony grabbed Rocki's hand when she stepped around him, pulled her behind him, and put away his gun. "If you hurt her, you're a dead man."

Darrell smiled in satisfaction and remained silent. Rocki tried to step around Tony again, and he pulled her to his side, his hand at her hip, keeping her away from Darrell.

"He wants to bargain," she whispered.

"She's cute. You do know that, right?" Darrell said, crossing his arms.

Cute. Maddening. Stubborn. And in so much trouble, he couldn't even look at her right now.

"Talk," Tony said.

"Like I told Camilla—excuse me, Rocki—I have information that could blow a hole in the police department and bring instant fame to your woman." Darrell held his hand up, stopping Tony from telling him to shut the hell up. "The only thing she has to do is drop her pursuit of me, and bury the evidence she's gathered in the last four months. It's quite simple. I get what I want and you get the girl. She makes a career move that would never happen to the fairer sex without someone handing her a deal like this one, and I stay clean. She makes herself a hero, earning the much-coveted lead detective position. Her mother remains safe and proud of her only daughter for the work she does protecting innocent citizens."

Rocki jolted. He tightened his grip on her to keep her beside him. That offer was not what he'd expected Darrell to put on the table.

"You pig," Rocki whispered. "I can't believe he went there."

"When you realize what I can do for you, I believe you'll think differently of me," Darrell said, sighing loudly. "Life can get complicated. Deals are made every day to…smooth the way."

"Jesus," Tony muttered. "What's the information?"

"Information comes after Rocki agrees to the deal." Darrell put his foot down, walked across the room to the bar, and poured himself two fingers' worth of whiskey. "If we strike no deal, you do realize I will have no other option than to make sure the information she holds never makes it to the bureau."

"And what happens if Rocki doesn't have enough information or the right kind of information on you to make the deal?" Tony said. "Are you going to kill us?"

Darrell bobbed his head side to side. "Of course she has the information. The question is, has she shared her newfound knowledge she gained working undercover for me with her lover or my nephew Kage?"

"Keep Kage out of this." Tony stared him down. "Or is this your way of saying that whatever we decide, you'll take the punishment out on your nephew?"

Darrell shrugged. "That depends on you...and Rocki, of course."

Rocki and Tony turned away from Darrell. She squeezed Tony's arm. "I know you have history with Darrell, but let me handle this."

"What information does Darrell have?" he asked.

Rocki glanced at Darrell and lowered her voice. "I don't know all of it, but if it has to do with the police department, maybe Gino's involved. I think I should take the deal. It'll at least buy us some time."

"You believe you'll be safe?" He lowered his head and whispered in her ear. "Put aside the idea of a promotion. Think with every bit of training you have. This is Darrell Archer we're dealing with. He's in a tight spot and will do and say anything to get his way. I don't trust him not to shoot us in the back as we walk out of the room. You can't put your confidence in him keeping his word."

She nodded. "I know, but I have a feeling what he'll give me will have some sort of truth to it. It'll at least give me an idea where to start searching for the facts. I can put him away for at least five to ten years right now with the information I have on him. He knows that."

Stuck between wanting to end the danger toward Rocki and

avoiding any agreement with Darrel, he studied the man who held the power in the room. Even looking at Darrell pissed him off. His sense of entitlement came off cocky, and Tony wanted nothing more than to walk away from the offer to show Darrell justice through the proper channels.

Tony motioned Rocki to follow him to the other side of the room. "Listen, you know how to proceed with Darrell, but I have one request. Do not involve Kage no matter what Darrell says. He only wants Kage under his thumb, back in the drug business, and I will not have Kage involved with Darrell."

"I don't know what Darrell will pull." Rocki moistened her lips. "But I won't involve you or Kage."

He nodded. "Okay. I trust you."

Her eyes widened and she tilted her head. He hooked her neck, bringing her closer. "Don't take chances, though, and if I see things heading south, I will step in."

"Yeah." She blinked up at him. "Thank you."

"Right." He studied Rocki. Owing Darrell sat wrong.

Taking Darrell down to keep Rocki safe would require a miracle. It wasn't only Kage's uncle, but his men he'd have to worry about coming after her. Darrell had a long reach in the underground, even if sent to prison.

"Let's do it," Rocki whispered, and turned around to face Darrell. "Let's talk."

"Fine." Darrell walked over and opened the door. "First let me guarantee that your friends will enjoy their evening without someone standing at their backs, that way we won't be interrupted."

One of his thugs stood on the other side in the hallway. They shared words, and then Darrell closed the door. Tony stood to the right of Rocki, making sure she was out of range should he have to go for his pistol.

Darrell stepped over and picked up the shot glass, but Tony caught on that he never actually drank from the cup. "To be up-front, I'll hold a marker on each of you after I divulge the information I have. You should be aware that at any time I could pull that marker. Seeing as how you're not from my world, I'll let you know a marker can either save your life or end it."

Tony ground his teeth together and nodded. He'd figure out how to deal with being at Darrell's beck and call after he heard what he had to say. The consequences would be dealt with later.

Darrell waited for Rocki to acknowledge the deal, and then continued. "Gino Marcelli has worked the areas of Cannon and Mansita for the last five years. Prior to that, I can vouch he's worked the streets for the last twenty years in Bay City. He brings in the dealers and offers them protection under the use of his badge. He cuts them a job, guaranteeing they'll never see jail time, and resells the deliveries." Darrell paused. "I'm talking pure."

Tony cocked his head. "Explain."

"This doesn't go outside of the room," Darrell said.

"Agreed," he said quickly. If he suspected Marcelli was responsible for the concentrated heroin making its way through bordering cities and could pin him in the recent deaths he'd heard about, this was big. Closing down the ring responsible for the pure heroin and taking the drug out of the hands of drug shooters would save more lives.

Darrell finally tossed back his first shot without even a flinch as he let the liquid burn down his throat. "To push Gino out of Bay City, off my territory, I bought him out years ago. I got the boundaries and his runners in the deal. It took every bit of money and disposable property I had at the time to clean out his supplies and pay off his people. The cut of heroin at the time was pure and the price was high. It set me back years, and this was after the FTA shut me down and I escaped the area for two years. Of course, at the time, I never knew how pure the cut was until it was too late."

"You don't sample your own product?" Rocki asked.

He shook his head. "No. Unfortunately my sister in law took the job of testing new shipments back then—despite everyone in the family urging her to go clean and rely on me and my brother to set up distribution."

Tony swallowed, and his heart raced. "You're saying it wasn't—"

"That's exactly what I'm saying. The night Kage's mother died, she was sampling Marcelli's surplus, not mine." Darrell held his gaze. "Remember your promise. This does not go out of the room."

"Fuck." He looked away. "Kage has a right to know."

"Do I need to remind you that I will kill you both before you can take one step toward the exit?" Darrell murmured.

He shook his head in disbelief. All these years, Kage held his uncle responsible, and it was Marcelli who gave her the blow that killed her. "Why?"

Darrell's smile didn't reach his eyes. "The timing is never right."

The air grew static. His chest tightened and he shifted toward Rocki, needing to see the truth in someone else's eyes to believe what he was hearing. She wrapped her arm around his waist and gazed up at him. How could he keep that type of life-changing information away from Kage? He deserved to know how his mother died. To keep believing his uncle injected her with the drug that killed her, when that wasn't true, was beyond cruel. He swung his gaze to Darrell. What did he gain from keeping this secret from Kage all these years when everyone knew Kage struggled over his mother's involvement in the drug world? Kage fought to outrun the past every day. The truth would be a big fucking deal.

"We need proof," Tony said.

Darrell walked around his desk, removed a key from his pocket, and opened the bottom desk drawer. Tony stepped forward and accepted the large manila envelope Darrell held toward him.

"Of course, you'll find no incriminating evidence against my involvement or what I've shared with you in this room today. What you will find are names, locations, and a tape with Marcelli willingly admitting to the drug run that killed Kage's mother and five others within a six-week span." Darrell sat down as if he couldn't hold himself up any longer, despite the man being in excellent shape.

Tony ran his hand down his jaw, trying to absorb all that he'd heard. "Then the truth will eventually come out. Why wouldn't you want to tell Kage yourself?"

Darrell sighed deeply and met his gaze. "That's between my nephew and me. You two struck a deal with me today. You owe me."

Rocki rubbed his back. He stared at Darrell, not ready to drop the subject. They were talking about Kage. His best friend deserved to know the man he blamed for his mother's death was not the one responsible.

More important, why would Darrell ruin his relationship with his only living family member to keep Marcelli's secret? The room squeezed in on Tony, and he shook his head in disgust.

This deal was more about family dynamics than Darrell's freedom. Rocki was a pawn in Darrell's sick game, and he'd used Tony to make sure Kage never found out the truth. The man disgusted him.

"Let's go, Tony," Rocki whispered. "We have everything we need."

He nodded and walked to the door. With his hand on the knob, he glanced behind him at Darrell, who'd swiveled his chair so he had his back to them. He tamped down the anger, unable to figure Darrell out, and walked out into the hallway.

Through all the wonderings about what just happened in that

room and the effect it would have on all of them before this case was over with, he concentrated on one thing: Rocki.

She'd held up during the talk and he'd caught himself forgetting that she was a successful detective and academy teacher, and not only his woman, even though Darrell knew the topic of discussion came more at a price for Tony than for Rocki. He glanced down at her and caught her hand, giving it a squeeze. Crazy as it seemed, while he was bargaining with their lives, one thing stood out blatantly clear. Rocki had called him Tony.

Chapter Sixteen

Scary intense and refusing to talk on the way home, Tony locked himself in one of his spare bedrooms the minute after arriving home and securing the house. Rocki turned the door handle again for the fifth time in the last hour to see if he would allow her inside. She'd gone from angry to frustrated to worried.

The inside information Darrell gave her wasn't what she was expecting. Deep down, she held on to hope there was a reasonable explanation regarding Gino's questionable behavior and her instincts. The last year, she'd studied, trained, and breathed the Archer case.

Every scenario possible of what could go wrong ran through her mind. She'd played the part for four months, and Darrell had blindsided her when she'd least expected it. Not once during her job had she suspected Gino of being a dirty cop. Gino, a detective, one of the highest supervisors in the department, running the incoming drug trade in the towns surrounding Bay City? The thought was unfathomable.

She needed to go over the logistics with someone and right now and Tony was the only person she trusted. She chewed on the edge of her lip. She hated to admit it, but she had no idea what her next step should be. All of her training pushed her toward informing the department. If she couldn't trust Gino, then she could go directly to the board and bring forth her allegations to open a new investigation.

The move would put a black mark against her. Men and women in the department would pull back, call her a rat, and alienate her from their support. Gino was one of the most respected detectives in the whole county.

"Weston." She rapped the door. "Please. Open the door."

She'd dealt with standoffs before, but this was personal. Something happened while they were dealing with Darrell that shifted the focus off the evidence she now held against Gino and straight to Tony's relationship with Kage. After the meeting, Tony declined the other guys' offer to go back to the body shop and talk over what went down at the Crystal Palace. He also refused to talk to her. She had no idea why he'd shut down and locked himself away from everyone.

She walked away, changed her mind, and returned to the door. "Okay, we won't talk. Just open up, so I can see if you're all right." She waited and when nothing happened, she laid her hand flat on the door. "Tony? Please."

The door opened, Tony pulled her into the room. She held on to his shoulders as he moved her faster than she could process to the wall. Plastered between the hard surface and his equally hard chest, she'd opened her mouth to ask him what was going on when he kissed her.

Hard.

Passionate.

Demanding.

He wrapped his hand around her hair and pulled away, holding her in place. He gazed into her eyes, watching, waiting, and seeking something basic and primal. The intensity in which he looked at her, standing in front of him, hit her low in the stomach and she melted.

"Tony," she whispered, raising her hand his cheek.

"Sorry, sweetheart," he whispered back. "It's your life we're playing with. Kage's life. It's fucked up. I needed to punch the bag. Didn't want you to deal with me the way I was…messed up."

She glanced over his shoulder, took in the exercise equipment, the weights, the punching bag. Understanding came, and she lifted her hand, cupping his cheek.

"I can handle you, Weston. Here and out there," she said.

"Then say my name." He tugged on her hair. "I don't know what stops you, but I need that from you. I want my name on your tongue, all the time. Can you give me that?"

She moistened her lips and took a shuddering breath. "Okay."

His own lips went to her neck and the fingers on his other hand dug into her hip, pulling the shirt she was wearing higher. When his hand hit bare skin, his head came up.

To strip down and put on his T-shirt when they got home, leaving her panties off, her breasts free, had been a rash decision on her part. Delighted over surprising him, she shrugged. "I was hoping…you know, we could be together again."

"Right," he mumbled.

He wrapped her arms around his neck, his hands moved to his belt. "You don't have to wish, sweetheart. It's a given. Me. You. You calling me Tony. This is us, and it isn't going away."

The metal clink of his buckle hitting his zipper thrilled her, but his words pleased her. She widened her legs as he lifted her up and pressed her against the wall, putting his hands flat against her back to protect her spine.

Then she slowly settled onto his hardness, wrapping her legs around his waist. She moaned as pleasure flooded her body. Possessed by his strength, his power, and put in the position to accept everything he asked for, her body ignited instantly.

"Damn." He growled, burying his head in her neck. "You're ready for me. So hot and tight."

He pulled out and thrust back in. She sucked in her breath. Her body spiraled tighter.

He didn't look frustrated or upset anymore.

He looked hot and possessive.

And she liked it. A lot.

He held himself still. "Say it."

She heard his swallow, felt his body shudder, and sensed his struggle to keep control. With her hands sunk deep in his hair, his body holding her against the wall, she could only give him what he needed. What she needed too.

"Tony," she whispered.

"Damn right." He grinned sexily. "I like when you say my name."

Her neck arched as he stroked her with his length. She locked her ankles behind his back, trying to match his movements and in the end, letting him take her to paradise. There were so many things she wanted to tell him. She could no longer ignore what was happening between them.

"Tony?" She moaned. "Thank you."

"Never had a woman I wanted more. Every day, you were in my head, and then you were there looking beautiful and full of shit, trying to beat me at pool, acting cool"—he grunted, plunging deep inside her—"being adorable."

"Oh God."

Could this get any better? "Please," she begged.

"So strong. Fucking gorgeous. Sweet and cute trying to be someone you're not, lying every time you opened your mouth, but I knew." His head came up and his eyes pierced hers. "Dammit, sweetheart, I knew you belonged to me."

Suddenly, his face dipped close, and he filled her vision. "Come for me."

And come for him, she did, squeezing him as pleasure curled and exploded from her center.

He arched, sinking to the root and holding himself stiff as he climaxed. She laid her head on his shoulder, letting him take all of her weight. She couldn't move. Didn't *want* to move. Ever.

When Tony caught his breath, he set her on her feet. She gazed up at him, and his smile went to somewhere she'd never seen from him before and didn't recognize.

"What?" She placed her hands on his stomach, grasping his shirt, and holding him in front of her.

"Shit," he muttered, pulling away and running his hands through his hair. "I lost it. I never lose control."

"I understand." She tilted her head and studied him. "Really. Stress and pressure build up inside of us differently, and—"

He faced her. "I didn't grab a condom."

"That's why you're upset?" When he nodded, she swallowed her amusement. That sealed it. Tony Weston was the last of the decent guys in the world. "It's okay. I'm on the pill."

His exhale came out in a rush. She moved toward him, kissed his chin, grinning because he looked relieved. For him to forget meant he was feeling the same obsessive need to be close to her that she was experiencing. That unrestrained hunger overtook her every time he was near. "Thank you."

"For?" He rubbed her arms.

"For being you. For caring about me. For having my back. For not walking away after I lied to you, broke into your house, and almost lost your dog," she whispered. "For making me understand that there are good guys still out there willing to help me and do good for others, for making me feel special even though we hardly know each other in a normal way, for showing me—"

"Got it, sweetheart." He chuckled.

She sighed happily. "Good."

He took her hand and led her to the bedroom. After she went to the bathroom, she let him tuck her into bed.

He hovered over her, kissed her quickly, and said, "I need to let Brute outside to run."

"Hurry back," she said, snuggling down under the comforter.

She listened to him walk through the house. Brute woofed. She smiled, loving the sound of Tony's life, his home, his dog. Now that she was no longer in danger, she wanted to help walk Brute and go jogging with Tony. Her stomach warmed. *Tony.*

For the first time she allowed herself to think about what being Tony Weston's girlfriend meant. A new relationship, a new boyfriend, and plenty of time to discover more ways to surprise him in the future eased the stress of the last six hours. She curled her legs and buried her head in the pillow. Once she took the evidence on Gino's dirty work to the bureau, she could concentrate on Tony.

Disgust and disappointment came every time she thought about Gino. She'd trusted him. She'd looked up to him. Yet he represented the exact kind of person she went after every day.

She closed her eyes and mind. Tomorrow, she'd deal with the repercussions of bringing down the head of the detective's department. Then she'd bring her mom home. Once her responsibilities were over, she'd allow herself to think about where she and Tony were headed in the relationship department.

Chapter Seventeen

The garage part of Beaumont Body Shop fascinated Rocki with all the tools and machinery at her disposal. Rocki poked at a rubber hose. Tony was right. They both needed time today to wrap their head around everything happening before they delivered the evidence Darrell gave them to the bureau.

She needed something to distract her, because she'd spilled her coffee at breakfast, blown up at Tony over a bad hair day, and forced Brute to put up with her extralong hug before she opened the can of dog food. On the verge of either crying or kicking someone—preferably Gino—Tony told her to get dressed and suggested they hang out at the body shop for the day.

Tony wanted to get his mind off what to do about Kage, and she wanted to forget how much Gino disappointed her. She rubbed at the spot of grease on the back of her hand. For how much the police department supported their own, bringing allegations against one another was almost unheard of.

Gino had friends in the department. She had friends in the department. All of their relationships would be tested before any decision was made by the court. And that's only if she delivered a believable case and the evidence panned out.

For today, she wanted to do something normal like hang out with Tony. Forget about what sat in front of her, and her duty to serve and protect. She sighed. She could no more shirk her responsibilities than stand back and watch Gino get away with murder.

After barely getting any sleep last night, she became more confused and worried as time passed. Everything came to an emotional meltdown this morning.

Yet she couldn't ignore her current problem, no matter how interesting and distracting she found the car business. She loved her job, and she was good at it.

Not only was she putting her own job at risk, because of the months she'd spent with Darrell, the board members would doubt her story. Maybe even believe she'd turned dirty, preferring fast money and the crime life over protecting innocent citizens and doing honorable work.

Rocki lay stretched across the engine on what Tony said was a classic Torino and pointed at a small black box hidden below what he called the cylinder. "What's that?"

Under the car on a wheelie board thingy, Tony rolled to the left and peered up to where she pointed. "The starter box."

She squeezed a black wire, spotted a flower-looking metal part, and stuck her head down farther. "What's this called?"

"It's a custom horn." Tony chuckled, and disappeared out of her line of vision.

All she could do was remind herself she wasn't alone. Tony had her back. She could go forward and present her case to her superiors, knowing he supported her. His protection helped but didn't take away her guilt at pressing charges against one of her own. Would the board believe her, even with the proof?

Everyone knew from the start of her career, even when she at-
tended the academy, she aimed for the position of top detective, and
her focus never swayed. None of the other female detectives had
gone as far as she had.

Despite the department being an equal opportunity employer,
she knew the unspoken rules and fought harder to prove herself every step of the way. Much to the amusement and, she suspected, the
chagrin of the men, they respected her.

She fiddled with a black wire. "What does this do?"

Tony scooped her off the car. She screamed, grabbing his shoulders. He stood her on the floor and rubbed the back of his hand
against her cheek. "You're a beautiful sight, pretending to enjoy
working on the car when you're keyed up tighter than a newly installed fan belt."

"Hey…I like watching you work. It's interesting." She wiped her
hands on the front of the coveralls Tony helped her pull on earlier
so she wouldn't get her clothes greasy.

"Sexy." He growled, wiggling his brows.

"Sure, I am. I'm covered in grease and wearing this thing that's ten
sizes too big."

He pulled her to his chest. "I like the smell of grease on you."

She shook her head, amused by him. "You're sick, Weston." She
paused. "Do you think if I brought my Honda here, you could
change the timing belt and I could watch? I'd pay you, and—"

His arms came around her and he bent her backward, kissing
away the rest of her words. When he came up for air, he said, "You're
not paying. I'll do your timing belt, and I'll even let you help, but if
I hear you call me Weston again, the deal's off."

She held on to his shoulders as he whipped her into a standing
position. She continued holding him, grinning. "Okay."

"Always testing me," he mumbled, unzipping the front of her coveralls. "When are you going to get it? You're my woman."

"I'm getting that." She grew serious. "Can I ask you one more question?"

He growled, but his eyes softened. She raised his arm.

She pointed to his tattoo. "Why a naked woman?"

"Why not?" he asked back.

"It's badass, but you do realize the one-colored ink and style means it was done by someone who has spent time in prison or has connections with those inside," she said.

"I know that, sweetheart." He shrugged. "I was investigating a guy for delinquency on past child support payments. He was getting a tattoo, so I sat down in the next chair and asked for my own tattoo while I discovered where the guy lived and worked."

"But a woman?" She arched her brow. "Is she an old girlfriend or your version of a pinup centerfold like the ones all over the garage?"

He shook his head. "I told you before, I saw you almost a year ago…It's you."

"Get out!" She backed away, shaking her head. No fricking way. He did not just say he marked his body with her likeness. Who did that sort of thing?

"What?" He held out his arm. "Don't you think it looks like you?"

She studied the tattoo, creeping closer to Tony. Upside down, the tattoo looked nothing like her. The hair flowed out to the sides, the slim hips, and the enormous—she slapped his shoulder. "Get out!"

He chuckled. "I told you. It even has the tiny mole by your eyebrow."

There was definitely a dot in the exact same spot as hers. She reached up and swept her finger over her brow, and even though she couldn't feel the brown mark, it was there.

She thought nothing would surprise her about Tony, but the tattoo…yeah, that was hot. She sagged against him. "It's really me?"

"Tattoo doesn't lie." He kissed her quick. "Let's clean up. I can't do any more with you here, asking so many questions, and talking to me."

"You're the coolest, most badass tattoo-wearing PI-slash-mechanic ever." She couldn't stop the grin. "Me…a tattoo."

"Only you in my head and on my body, sweetheart," he mumbled.

"I like it." She kissed him hard. "A lot."

He slapped her ass. "Enough to stop calling me Weston?"

"Maybe…" She leaned into him as she wiggled her arms out of the sleeves. He held her hand, and she stepped out of the legs. "Don't forget we need to be at the academy at five o'clock to meet with Detective Hanara and Officer Bailey."

"I know." He wadded up the coveralls and threw them on the bench. "Go ahead and use the guys' bathroom in the back. Put the sign up so none of the guys will walk in on you. I want to talk with Kage, and then I'll meet you in headquarters. Make sure you stay in the building."

She stilled and watched him. When he looked away, she caught the worry etched around his eyes. She moved toward him.

"Tony?" She laid her hand along his jaw.

His gaze moved away from her. "What?"

As she lay in his arms last night, listening to him go through the choices he had to make, her opinion of him solidified. He'd explained what Kage believed happened to his mother, and how the truth could set him free. Tony's guilt at holding on to information that could change his friend's life ate away at him.

Tony Weston was one of the good guys. The best. Upstanding, morally responsible, and full of more integrity than any man she knew. And she realized she was falling madly in love with him.

She gave a short shake of her head, leaned in and kissed him lightly. "Okay, gorgeous. I'll be safe."

"Gorgeous?"

"Yeah," she whispered. "It's better than calling you Weston and making you mad, huh?"

His mouth softened. "Go clean up before I lean you over the Torino and ruin the new paint job."

She gazed at the car, wondering exactly how and what he'd do to her. Intrigued, she raked her teeth over her bottom lip. She was just the right height to...

He burst out laughing. "Come on, sweetheart."

She grabbed his shirt. "Can we—"

He patted her bottom. "Go. Before your naughty thoughts get us both in trouble."

"All right. All right. You don't have to get bossy with me," she said, rubbing the side of her butt as she walked out of the garage.

Chapter Eighteen

Inside the weight room, Kage sat backward on the bench in front of the press and hung his arms over the bar. Tony stood beside the pull-down bar opposite him, and shoved his hands in his front pockets. How was he supposed to bring up a subject Kage refused to talk about?

They'd grown up together. The history between them went clear back to kindergarten, when his mom had felt sorry for Kage, who walked to school alone, without a parent by his side, and taken Kage under her wing. Thank God she had.

For reasons Tony never thought about until he was an adult, he'd latched on to Kage from that day forward. Maybe he knew his friend needed someone, or that Kage was so fucking cool he wanted to spend time with him, but he'd never questioned his friendship. Hell, he looked up to Kage.

Despite being the same age, Kage seemed years older and a decade wiser.

Now, he had information that would change Kage's life, and he gave his word on Rocki's life, that he wouldn't share the news with his best friend. What kind of friend did that?

"Are you going to talk?" Kage asked.

Tony sat on the incline bench, bracing his boots on the floor. "I've got a problem. I'm not sure how to fix it or if I should do something about it."

"Figured that's why you called me to come here." Kage sighed deeply and lowered his voice. "Is this about Rocki?"

He shook his head. "No, things are good between us. Better than I expected considering the shit we're going through and how we met."

"Then what?" Kage asked.

He had no idea how to explain the situation. Kage was smart; he'd read through any lie, and Tony would insult their relationship with anything but the truth. He damned Darrell Archer to hell, and said, "Last night at the Crystal Palace, when we dealt with Darrell, he gave us information that affects you, but I gave my word to your uncle that I'd keep it to myself for the time being."

Kage relaxed and shrugged. "If it came from my uncle, whatever he said to the both of you means nothing to me. Don't sweat it."

"You'd want to know, bro." Tony stood and walked over to the punching bag, tapped it twice with his fist. "The hell of it is I'm protecting Rocki by not telling you and that doesn't set right with me either. I agreed on keeping my silence to strike a deal with Darrell and keep his men off Rocki. It was either that or protect her for the rest of her life, and we both know that's a hell of a life for anyone. You're continually on guard, and though you don't say anything, I realize the damage that was done because of your connection to the Archer name."

"She's your woman. I don't see what the big deal is or why you have to worry about me. I live my own life. What Darrell does and continues to do has no reflection on me," Kage said.

His friend's openness and unguarded reaction bothered him. He got what he was saying, but the unfairness of it all angered him. Kage had given up a lifetime of doing what he wanted, when he wanted, and with whom he wanted, to make sure no one mistook his actions and brought trouble down on him, Janie, and the agency. A lesser man would've caved.

"I know how you feel, but you and I both know that everyone in this town will link you two together no matter if it's me or one of the other guys who have to deal with him. The citizens of Bay City are accepting but leery…I can understand, because most of them realize there is someone more powerful running their town than the mayor. The drug trade is a big deal here, and everyone wants a clean town. You can't outrun your family name, and they'll speculate how you're involved. I respect the hell out of you for making sure nothing reflects on your integrity, and I'll admit that if roles were reversed, I doubt if I'd have the strength to stand strong as long as you have. This situation…it's fucking unfair. It's personal, and my instinct is to keep you away from the fallout." He ran his hand over his forehead. His temples pounded from the weight of his involvement.

He'd stayed awake, lying in bed last night when he wasn't making love to Rocki, thinking about nothing else but what he'd do with his secret. Keeping his mouth shut bought Rocki more time. She wasn't out of danger. He wasn't stupid. He agreed with Darrell. The information given to Rocki was too big of a package to ignore.

But so was a lifetime friendship with one of the few men he trusted with his life. He closed his eyes for an extra beat. He couldn't keep his word. Kage's well-being meant more to him than staying honest with a drug lord. Together, they could protect Rocki for however long it took.

"Listen, man. If it were Janie, I'd do whatever I had to do to keep her safe. Hell, I did when her ex-boyfriend came after her. I was willing to go maverick and turn my back on everything I believed in because I loved her. I learned everyone has limits and Janie's mine. There's nothing I wouldn't do to keep her in my bed, in my life, and alive. I'd kill for her, man."

Tony nodded, because he understood. Despite having known Rocki for only a week, he'd thought, dreamt, and wanted her for much longer. Having her personally in his life was better than he ever imagined. The level he'd go to keep what was his scared him. Because not once did he ever think he'd push aside his friendship with Kage for a woman.

"I want you to know that Rocki's it for me, like Janie is for you. She's the one," he said.

"Okay." Kage joined him at the bag and held the weight while Tony put some power behind a swing.

They stayed in position. Tony hit left, right, high, low, and Kage took the brunt of the force being his spotter. He put his frustrations on the bag, trying to knock some sense into his responsibilities, as if he could beat back the fear and know in his heart he was doing the right thing for everyone involved.

After a few minutes, Tony stopped. The situation was clear. He could do both. Somehow, he'd make Kage understand and keep Rocki safe. There was only one thing he could do. He had to tell him the truth, because above all else, he wasn't going to sink to Darrell's level. He'd shoot straight and believe that doing the right thing paid off in the long run.

"You need to know," he said.

Kage straightened. His mouth grew tense and he looked at the ceiling before meeting Tony's eyes. "Just answer me this before you say anything you'll regret. Does it involve Janie?"

"No."

"Will Janie be put in danger if I don't know what's going on?" Kage asked quietly.

"No." Tony inhaled deeply. "This affects you personally. Even though I gave my word—and, dammit, you know I don't give that unless I mean it—my loyalty is to you. Not your uncle. Keeping this from you makes me sink down to his level, and I couldn't live with myself for turning my back on you."

"Keep your word, man." Kage punched his shoulder and turned to walk away.

His body went solid. "Just like that, you're fine with everything?"

Kage raised his hand without turning around or stopping. "Just like that."

"Fuck that, Kage," he muttered.

Kage laughed, but the sound was loose and given freely, it was accepting. Tony stood there, staring at Kage until the door shut, blocking his view. Then he clenched his hand and sent the punching bag swinging.

If anyone wanted to know what a real man looked like, he just walked out the door. Tony checked his watch. Almost time to bring war down on the bureau. He wished he could keep the mess from touching Rocki, but she was smack-dab in the middle. All he could do was stay with her, support her.

They headed to her place to pick up her clothes for the meeting. He could tell how worried she was. And he would stick beside her. He blew out his breath. She was strong and smart. Everything would be okay.

Chapter Nineteen

In her official navy-colored dress skirt and coat and white blouse, Rocki paused outside the door to the boardroom at the academy. Her heels echoed in the stark hallway on the tiled floors. She tugged at the hem of her jacket and adjusted the tie at her neck. She was glad she had Tony come with her early to change out of her street clothes.

"You look great," Tony whispered. "Relax."

"My hands are shaking." She grabbed his arm and looked up at him. "It's been four months, and they have no idea what information I'm giving them."

She stepped around Tony and he snagged her hand. "Sweetheart, you're fine. "

"Okay." She nodded as her stomach flip-flopped. "I can do this."

He smiled tenderly at her. "Yeah. You can."

"They'll believe me, right?" She shook her head. "Don't answer. I'm being stupid. Justice always prevails, and I'm not the one who broke the law."

She tugged her hand, but he kept her from walking to the door. "What?"

"Breathe." He waited and when she took a short breath, he said, "Again."

All the while, he held her hand, his thumb stroking her knuckles. Her nerves settled into a hum rather than a screaming fit. Surprised to find herself more confident, she swallowed. "I got this. I can do it. I'll just walk in, tell them what I know, answer their questions, and it'll be over."

"Right." He stepped out of the way and opened the door for her.

She swept past him into the room. *Please don't let me fall apart.*

On the other side of the large boardroom, Detective Hanara stood from behind his desk, scowling in her direction. His bushy mustache hid his lips, but she knew he was displeased. His lowered eyebrows and tucked chin said everything she needed to know. On her right, Officer Bailey remained standing and tapped the heels of his thick black service shoes together as he straightened to his full height of six feet tall. She dipped her chin at each of them.

"Good evening, Detective Hanara and Officer Bailey. Thank you for agreeing to see me this evening on such short notice." She stood beside the chair in front of the desk at attention. "This is Tony Weston, a private investigator with the Beaumont Body Shop in Bay City. I've asked him to join us today because he's directly involved with the recent undercover case against Mr. Darrell Archer, also of Bay City, case number 2463A-C."

The men shook hands, and Detective Hanara motioned for them to sit. "Detective Marcelli reported that you removed yourself from the case because of high probability that Archer was on to your status with the department. Then I received a ten ninety-nine form for two weeks of vacation filed for you. Maybe we should start there, before I learn what happened during the four months we were paying you to gather information to bring down our suspect."

She folded her hands in her lap. "Detective Marcelli is correct.

Mr. Archer confronted me, willingly admitted to discovering my position as a detective for the Cannon Police Department, and wanted to know why I was working for him. I denied any involvement, and when he left me after the meeting, I feared for my safety and escaped."

"Yet, from the report, you went to Mr. Weston's house instead of contacting your commanding officer." Detective Hanara leaned back and steepled his fingers. "Highly against regulations, Detective Bangli."

The blow from his reprimand stung. She'd always gone by the book and followed procedures. Because of Gino's involvement, she'd relied on herself instead of the department's protection. Anger toward the man who'd taught her everything and overseen her training threatened to make her rise from the chair and tell them all she knew in one temperamental outburst, but she tamped the urge down.

"Correct, sir." She cleared her throat and removed the manila envelope from Tony's hands. "In my defense, I've received information that compromises Detective Marcelli's role as my superior and until I delivered the evidence into your hands, I made the decision not to release the information to Detective Marcelli. The truth is, sir, I was concerned with my safety if I took the package to Detective Marcelli. I believe the conflict of interest will be liable in court."

Detective Hanara tilted his head. "Think very carefully before you make any accusations that you can't back up and prove as fact, Detective Bangli."

Tony's body shifted forward. She put her hand on his thigh, assuring him she had the situation under control, and laid the envelope on the desk. "I'm requesting the board to open an investigation on Detective Gino Marcelli for illegal drug trade, blackmail, theft, and tampering with criminal evidence, going against everything the bureau believes in and using his position to conduct illegal activities. Along with being responsible for the deaths of six people, twenty years ago, five of those victims are cold cases that I can solve."

"You've got to be shitting me, Bangli." Detective Hanara came out of his chair and towered over his desk. "What is this bullshit?"

"The truth, sir. All the evidence is in the envelope," she said.

The air inside the room suffocated her. Her heart hammered against her chest. His reaction came as no surprise, but nothing could prepare her for the onslaught of guilt over accusing one of her own.

"May I ask where and who gave you the evidence you're bringing in front of the board?" he asked, his voice gravely serious.

Earlier, she'd talked to Tony about the best way to handle answering the question she knew would come up about Archer, and they'd both agreed. If she were to remain safe, she'd take responsibility and leave Archer's name out of her story. Okay, Tony didn't agree and they'd fought, but in the end, he'd remained silent, letting her make the decision on her own.

The police department used informants all the time. Archer was working with her.

"I gathered it while I working undercover." She pulled her shoulders back. Always truthful; if she kept information to herself, it wasn't lying. "The physical evidence, the recordings, and the pictures were handed to me personally for payment on the jobs I fulfilled while on duty for the Cannon Police Department."

"Shit." Officer Bailey bent at the waist and braced his elbows on his knees.

Rocki kept her gaze forward, allowing the officer time to collect himself. News of a scandal this big would rock the town of Cannon for many years, and he deserved enough time to grasp what she was telling them. The lives of every single person employed by the bureau would be tested, talked about, and run through internal affairs. None of them would walk away without feeling the effects of Detective Marcelli's actions.

Detective Hanara studied her for several seconds and turned to Tony. "And your involvement?"

"I was with her while she was working undercover on the case, doing my own investigative work into Mr. Archer. I witnessed the exchange. She was given the package honestly. Because of my close involvement with the police in the county, I was aware of Detective Bangli's true identity from prior occasions while she worked here at the academy. I stayed around to make sure she remained safe." Tony remained sitting, his body relaxed to the others in the room, but she could sense the tension rolling off him. "When the job became too risky, I helped her stay out of sight until she could contact her superior. The first night before she could make contact with Detective Marcelli, we had a drive-by shooting at my place of residence, which resulted in the police being called and a report filed. Detective Marcelli came out of his jurisdiction to meet with Detective Bangli before he was notified she'd left the job."

"That doesn't mean anything." Officer Bailey tilted his head and looked down at Rocki. "His radio would pick up the nine one one call from dispatch. It's out of his jurisdiction, but we all know if extra help is needed, he serves not only Cannon, but the county as a whole."

"True." Rocki looked Officer Bailey in the eye. "And yet, since I've known him, he never responds to a call in the district's unmarked patrol car, wearing street clothes, during off hours."

Detective Hanara sat and shook his head. "Give us a few moments to figure out what we're dealing with, please."

Tony's hand covered hers. She swallowed. "I'm afraid we can't let the evidence out of our sight, sir. I want it reported, tagged, filed, and locked away in the evidence room to be copied and handed over to the department's lawyer. I will not chance having Detective Marcelli get his hands on the package."

"You do know what this will do to the department, to the academy, if what you're telling me is true?" Detective Hanara scowled.

She steeled her spine and refused to cower under his threat. "Yes, sir, I do."

Two hours later, Detective Hanara, Officer Bailey, Attorney Phil Armour, Tony, and two security guards escorted her from the file room. Then she listened as Detective Hanara put out an APB on Gino Marcelli.

Rocki led Tony out of the building. Her legs shook and she bent over to catch her breath, and Tony's arm hooked her waist, catching her. She leaned into him.

"Good job, sweetheart. A little bit farther and I'll take you to the house and you can deal with what went down in private," he murmured.

She climbed into the passenger seat of the Camaro, buckled, and sat quietly as Tony started the car and drove them off the academy's property. She stared out the windshield as they passed the Dairy Queen and the Cannon plaza, then drove onto the highway heading north to Bay City.

Tony remained silent, but offered her continual support by holding her hand. She squeezed his fingers, afraid if she let go, she'd crumble.

Once she found her voice, she'd thank him for supporting her at the meeting. She could tell it killed him not to defend and jump to her defense. Yet what he didn't know was that without his confidence in her, she would've backed down.

Despite their history she couldn't let Gino get away with what he'd done, even if bringing the allegations to the board cost her the promotion or her job.

Her door opened. She blinked up at Tony, unaware that they'd arrived at his house. She let him pull her out of the Camaro and into his arms. She buried her face in his neck. Against his warm skin, within his strong embrace, she let the worry and stress go.

Chapter Twenty

Brute lumbered out into the living room, stretched his massive legs, saw Rocki, and whined. As Rocki moved forward and hugged the dog, Tony locked the door and waited to set the alarm. Proud of the fight Rocki won today, he reluctantly left her to open the sliding door into the backyard.

He wanted everything secured for the rest of the night, because he wasn't planning to get out of bed until morning. "Come on, Brute. Let's go outside."

The dog remained in the front of the house.

"Brute. Come," he said.

Rocki brought Brute into the kitchen and pointed to the door. "Go potty."

His dog trotted toward him, paused, looked back at Rocki, and then gazed up at Tony before walking out onto the patio. He shook his head. The message was clear. Brute's concern over Rocki's tender hold on her emotions was even apparent to the dog.

"Got her covered, buddy," he whispered.

Tony stood with the door open, watching Rocki carefully. She gazed outside, deep in thought, probably over what had gone down in that boardroom at the academy. His job as a private investigator distanced him from the governing force she worked under and allowed him to see what was happening. She struggled with what she'd done. She'd turned in a shield, and guilt lay heavy on her shoulders.

"Sweetheart?"

Her gaze came to him. "Hmm?"

"You did the right thing."

She nodded. "I should probably call my mom."

He strode over and handed her his cell. "The number for their hotel is in there. You can make the call and give her the news. Your mom will want to know that you're all right. Tell her to let my dad know he can bring everyone home."

She leaned up on tiptoes and kissed his cheek. "Thanks, gorgeous."

The tension eased from his shoulders as she walked out of the room. He could get used to her being here, looking up at him, and talking to him in that soft voice she uses when they're alone.

After letting Brute inside, he set the alarm then checked in on Rocki in the living room to make sure she was doing all right. The one-sided conversation he caught was intense and heartbreaking. He left her to finish her call in privacy. No matter the age, a daughter needed her mom when dealing with a crisis.

In the meantime, he kicked the dirty clothes scattered around his bedroom into a pile, and then went into the bathroom and started the water flowing in the tub. Brute watched him from the doorway.

"Come on, buddy. Let's go find you a treat." He walked out of the bedroom and into the spare room down the hall.

On the top shelf of the closet, he removed one of the massive chew bones he kept out of Brute's reach and tossed it on the bed. Brute jumped on the mattress and went to town, working on the ends, happy to have a little attention. Tony sat down and gave him a big scratch behind his floppy ears.

"Won't be long before I'll be able to spend more time with you, take you for a run and let you ride to the garage with me on the weekends," he said. "The deal with Rocki will be over soon; until then Rocki's going to need me for a little bit longer."

Brute looked up, seemed to study the empty doorway as if hearing Rocki's name reminded him that she was in the other room alone, and then went back to chewing. He gave the dog a final pat and left to check the water level in the tub.

After shutting off the faucet, he met Rocki coming into the bedroom. He held out his hand, and she walked to him. Red-rimmed eyes gazed at him and she sniffled.

"Everything okay with your mom?" he asked.

"Yeah." She kicked off her heels. "I tried to talk her into waiting until tomorrow to fly home, but Mom wanted to leave right away. Your dad was calling for tickets as I said good-bye."

"She's worried. My dad probably knew she wouldn't relax until she could see you for herself and know that you're okay."

She stepped away and sat on the bed. "I know. I've always tried to protect her from what happens at work. Going undercover and dealing with Archer afterward, well, I think she's realized how dangerous my job can be and she's scared for me."

"You're a detective. A damn good one," he whispered. "You can't protect her forever."

Her gaze snapped to him in the middle of taking off her bracelet. "I know that. I've even taken her to self-defense classes and the firing range, so she could protect herself when I'm not around. It's just...she's my mom and she seems to think there's only good in the world. I don't want to shatter her illusion. I kind of want to keep her that way."

"I get that, sweetheart." He pulled the hem of her dress up. "And, I want to keep you happy, so you're going to get undressed and let me give you a bath."

"A bath, Weston?" She laughed.

He stilled. "What's that supposed to mean?"

"Oh, I don't know." She lifted her butt off the mattress and let him sweep her dress over her head. "Maybe it's because you're the strongest, most bullheaded man with the sexiest smile, the biggest—"

"Dick?" He grinned.

She snorted. "That too. But, I was going to say the biggest shoulders I've ever slept on. And now you're seducing me by giving me a bath, and"—she glanced at him—"I think I might be falling in love with you, Weston."

"Say it again, but drop the Weston." He hooked her waist and dragged her naked body against him.

Her arms wrapped around his neck. "I'm falling in love with you, Tony."

"About damn time, sweetheart." He scooped her up, and cradled her in his arms.

Tony carried her into the bathroom and put her in the bathtub. She sank to her shoulders into the water and closed her eyes. He stood ogling and thinking how beautiful and irresistible he found her.

"No bubbles?" She peeked up at him before closing her eyes again.

Shit. Girls like bubbles. Right. I can do bubbles.

He scoured the bathroom cabinets, and the only thing he could find was a half-empty bottle of Brute's flea and tick shampoo. He held the container toward the light, squinting at the writing on the side of the bottle when soft laughter drew his attention back to Rocki.

"I don't think so," she said.

He frowned. "It's nontoxic."

She laughed, and he threw the bottle into the sink. Without thinking, he shucked off his clothes. He might not be able to give her bubbles and candlelight, but he'd give her his attention.

Rocki's eyes came open when he stepped into the water. He grinned at the look of shock replaced by curiosity. A hiss came out between his clenched teeth as he sank down into the hot water, sending a wave over the rim of the tub onto the floor.

"You're going to get your floor soaking wet," she said.

He ignored the mess. "It'll be fine. We can throw our towels down when we're done."

She leaned forward, turning, and slid into the spot between his legs, resting her back against his front. "You're crazy, brilliant, and really big to share a bath with, you know."

"Lift your feet out of the tub," he whispered. "Maybe I'll remodel the bathroom. Bigger would be good."

She scooted down until the water touched her ears and lifted her feet. He palmed the top of her head and dunked her under the surface.

She came up sputtering. "Real classy, Weston."

"Hang on. It'll get better."

He grabbed the shampoo bottle—the human kind—and squirted a good-sized dollop in her hair. Her body softened and she let her head fall back on his chest. He used the tips of his fingers and massaged her scalp. Lather grew and he flicked his hands in front of her, sending a spray of bubbles on top of the water. He could do bubbles.

She laughed softly. "Perfect."

He spread the length of her hair out on the water, taking care to shampoo each strand. The blackness in her hair darkened with the water, and he diligently separated a strand. He'd never been this intimate with a woman before...never had one stay over, much less run a bath and bathe her before. He smiled, contentment washing over him. He loved having Rocki in his life.

She slowed him down, and made him appreciate the beauty that came along with having a woman in the house. Everything she did fascinated him.

He was a wash-and-shake-dry guy. Rocki styled hers, spending hardly any time, and came away looking ball-achingly gorgeous. A natural beauty, she could slap on a baseball hat and he'd still want her.

A low, feminine moan filled the bathroom. His body hardened and he bent his neck to kiss her wet forehead. "Good?"

"Wonderful," she mumbled.

"Close your eyes." He worked the shampoo around her face. "Hold your breath."

He warned her this time and she went under the water on her own. He used his hands and quickly worked the soap out of her hair. When she came up for air, he realized that in his hurry to get in the tub and get naked, he'd forgotten the towels.

"Scoot up, sweetheart. I need to get us some towels."

She rubbed her hands over her face, turned, and blinked rapidly up at him. "You're kidding."

"No. I forgot to set some out," he said.

She rolled her eyes. "You have a lot to learn about women."

Before he could ask her what she was talking about, she pulled herself to her feet, flipped the stopper lever to open, and turned on the shower. From his spot below her, he eyed her body until a faceful of spray shot down on him.

She grabbed his hand. "On your feet, big guy. Let me show you how women like to wash, because we never stop at only a bath and call it good. We like to wash off with clean water."

He proceeded to stand there and watch her put conditioner in her hair. He groaned, rubbing his abdomen as her head went back, exposing her slim neck, her breasts thrust higher. He laid his hands on her hips, riveted by the water drops rolling all over her.

"Hold out your hands," she said.

He shook his head. "Don't want to."

"Oh, trust me." She dropped her gaze to his chest. "You'll like this part."

She removed his hand, placed a bar of soap in his grasp, and gave him instructions to work up a good lather. When she deemed the job done, she raised her arms, and whispered for him to wash her.

It didn't take him long to learn he really loved how women took showers. He'd have to remember the rules. Shower after bath. Shampoo before conditioner. Soap on hands.

By the time he'd soaped up her legs, spent a considerable amount of time between her thighs and lower stomach, he was breathing hard and sporting an even harder erection. Rocki eyed him sleepily and planted her own soapy hands on his chest. He stood still, letting her spread the bubbles over his body. Pleasure and pain mingled as his cock hardened. When she lowered her hand, he grabbed her wrist, stopping her.

"Can't wait," he murmured, finishing the job of washing himself, spraying off under the water in record time. "That's how guys shower."

She laughed. "Dually noted."

He opened the glass sliding door, lunged out of the tub, and retrieved two towels, handing one to Rocki. After giving himself a few swipes to dry off, he flung the towel to the corner of the bathroom and led Rocki into the bedroom.

"Tony, my hair." She dragged her feet. "I need to comb the snarls out while it's wet.

"Leave it. I love snarls on you, sweetheart." He grasped her hips and lifted upward.

She screamed in surprise, threw her legs around his hips, and locked her hands behind his neck. Then he fell backward, holding her to him as his back hit the bed and Rocki landed square on top of him, where he wanted her.

"I want to be inside of you." He skimmed his hands up her thighs and watched her take his hardness in her hand before lowering herself on his length.

He groaned at the erotic sight, the warmth, and her body squeezing him. He raised his hands to her breasts. His thumbs honed in on her nipples, tweaking, rolling, and rubbing. He could die in the plushness of her breasts alone. The perfect shape more than filled his hands, and her hard nipples tempted him to taste her.

Even though he wanted to slow down, spend more attention on her, he knew Rocki was too tired for a drawn-out evening, no matter how much her beautiful brown eyes said differently. He wanted to relax her, not wear her out more. Despite the lax jaw, the heated gaze, he was struggling to keep the pace to please her.

He flipped her over and took top position, burying his mouth in her neck. "Hold on, sweetheart. We're going fast and big."

Then he fulfilled his promise.

She gasped when he cut off her next breath with a kiss. She quivered underneath him as he thrust. He muttered against her lips, "Unbelievable."

"Oh God…" Her rapid breaths caressed his cheek. Her hand came up to dive into his hair, holding him close.

"That's it, sweetheart." His voice rumbled through his body as he fought for control. "Take it all."

Never had he met a woman who reached in, grabbed his soul, and flourished every bit of her attention toward him, even when her own life was blowing up around her. One look and he wanted her. One touch and he wanted to possess her body. One whisper of her soft voice and he wanted to keep her forever.

She arched beneath him, her fingernails biting into his scalp. He rocked the bed, taking her higher until she shuddered, squeezing the life out of him. He buried himself to the root as pleasure consumed his entire body, curling his toes.

Unable to support his weight any longer, he rolled to the side, taking her with him. He tucked her under his chin, his hand possessively planted on her hip. And still he wanted her as close as he could get her.

Several minutes went by before Rocki had fallen asleep and he slipped out of her embrace to shut off the lights. Then he stalked back to the bed, dragging the covers over them both.

Rocki snuggled close. "Tony?"

"Go to sleep," he whispered. "Everything's okay."

She gave him a contented sigh. "Okay, gorgeous," she whispered back.

He closed his eyes, but couldn't stop the smile that came to his lips. Finally, they could concentrate on them, and move forward.

Chapter Twenty-One

A loud knock at the front door startled Rocki. She squealed, staring bug-eyed at Tony underneath her. It was six o'clock in the morning. Who visited that early?

Tony gripped her waist and set her beside him on the floor. He
tossed her the shirt he'd removed only moments ago. She shoved
her arms in the sleeves, grabbed her shorts off the floor, dressed, and
stood. She grabbed Tony as he walked across the living room. "Wait.
Your belt."

He stopped and buckled, tucking in his T-shirt. "Do me a favor
and hand me my pistol."

In a split second, he went from ravishing her to being seriously
cool. She stepped over to the end table, flipped the safety off, and
handed him the weapon. "It's live."

"Thanks." He kissed her quick and stalked to the door. Looking
through the peephole, he said, "It's Hanara."

"What could he want?" she whispered, slipping her finger
though the belt loop at the back of his jeans.

He glanced down at her. "I don't know, but I guess we're going to
find out."

For her supervisor to show up at Tony's house, out of his jurisdiction, was highly unusual when he could've called her phone. Tony opened the door and she stepped out from behind him.

"Detective," Tony said.

"Weston." Detective Hanara removed his hat and stepped inside. He turned his attention to Rocki. "I wanted to stop by and let you both know we were unsuccessful in locating Detective Marcelli. As of now, we have a warrant out for his arrest and every patrol officer on the lookout for him."

She stepped away and leaned into the back of the couch. "Have you talked to his wife?"

Detective Hanara nodded. "Yes, we talked to her late last night while we searched his house. We've asked her to come in for questioning this morning. A patrol car is picking her up at ten o'clock. She's let us know that her lawyer will be with her."

"I thought you'd get him as he went off duty last night." She pressed her hand to her forehead. "Where would he go?"

"That's the million-dollar question. Considering his contacts and the accusations, he could be hiding out or have flown the country. His evasion to our call doesn't reflect positively on the case building around him." Detective Hanara turned to Tony. "I wanted to come by personally and update you. It might be a wise decision to play it safe and stay together. Not only is Marcelli accused of breaking federal law, we're assuming he's dangerous until we bring him in. That's off the record, mind you."

"Sure," Tony murmured.

This couldn't be happening. Even though the evidence damned Gino to life in prison, she thought the bureau could jump on Gino before he became aware of the situation. She ground her teeth together. Somehow, he had someone on the inside, but who?

Every time she turned around, she found more disappointment

and illusions. She wanted him to pay. He'd not only broken the law, but also used her and their friendship.

She stood between Marcelli and time in prison, removal of his badge, and his dirty business. She rubbed her arm, working out the goose bumps. Of course he'd want to remove his one and only threat. With her out of the picture, Gino could destroy the evidence.

It would be her accusations against his experience, seniority, and past record. She hung her head and closed her eyes. They had to catch him.

Another loud *bang* jolted her out of her thoughts. She whipped her gaze toward Tony. He moved around Detective Hanara and checked the peephole.

"Jesus…" He opened the door.

A harried Pauline with her makeup smeared and hair in a mess entered with a frazzled and angry Caleb. Rocki moved toward Tony's mom, concerned over the tears trailing down her cheeks unchecked.

"Are you okay? Did you get in an accident?" She grabbed Pauline's hand.

Pauline shook her head, unable to look at her. Caleb's voice boomed. "We came right from the airport. You"—he swung his arm at his son—"need to come quick."

"Slow down, Dad." Tony eyed both his parents. "Tell me what's going on."

Caleb gazed at Rocki and his face softened. Rocki's heart pounded, a sinking feeling landing in her stomach. Something bad had happened.

"Oh my God. Where's my mom?" she said.

"We're not sure." Caleb shook his head. "We went to claim our luggage at the carousel at the airport and Mary needed to use the restroom. Since things had cooled off, Mary said she'd be all right going by herself and suggested we go ahead to retrieve our baggage and she'd meet us there. Honest, the bathroom doors were in sight the whole time and I thought she'd be safe. This is my fault."

"What happened?" Tony asked.

"Ten minutes went by and Mary never returned to us at luggage pickup. Pauline went to the bathroom looking for her." Caleb gazed intently at Tony.

"Please." Rocki's throat tightened. "Where is she?"

"Gone." Caleb threw his hands to the side of him in frustration. "We looked everywhere, and when we couldn't find her, we reported her missing with airport security and came right here. Tony's house was closer than going to the police department, and we knew he could find her. The damn airport personnel wanted us to wait twenty-four hours to report her as missing."

Rocki walked across the room. "I need to go." She whirled around. "It's either Darrell or Gino. I know it."

"Rocki, let's think for a second." Tony took her by the elbow until his back was to the others. "Darrell would be stupid to go after you now that he knows the heat is off him and aimed at Marcelli. He wouldn't do anything to jeopardize his freedom."

She frowned. "Then it's Gino."

"Yeah," he said. "I'd bet everything on him."

She stepped around Tony and hurried to the others. "I'm going after Marcelli."

Detective Hanara cussed under his breath. "Detective Bangli, I understand you have a personal vend—"

"It's my mother. I want a missing person report filed immediately with the bureau." She turned to Tony. "Will the guys at the body shop help us?"

"Absolutely. I'll call them now." Tony removed his cell phone from his pocket.

Rocki turned to Detective Hanara. "I'm asking permission to use all resources."

Hanara smacked his hat against his thigh. "Detective…"

"Sir, after what I've gone through the last four months and considering we're dealing with one of our own, I believe I'm owed this favor. Do not pull me off the case," she said.

Department rules favored anyone close or related to a suspect staying off the case. However, nobody would stop her from finding her mom. Although she'd prefer to keep her badge while looking for Mary, she'd set it down in a heartbeat to save her mother.

"Fine." Hanara moved toward the door. "Mr. and Mrs. Weston could you step outside? We'll fill out a report and get Ms. Bangli into the system. I'll need to know everything that happened."

Brute barked and trotted to Rocki's side. She sank her fingers into his fur. If there was one person who didn't deserve to go through a kidnapping, it was her mother. She probably had no idea that her life was in danger. God, she should've insisted her mom learn the whole truth of what was going down when they sent her to Hawaii. Mary had no idea what kind of people Rocki investigated on a daily basis or what could happen if she fell into the hands of those kinds of people.

"The guys are on their way." Tony held her gaze. "How are you holding up?"

She squared her shoulders. "Fine."

His gaze softened and he held out his hand, beckoning her to come to him. She shook her head and stayed where she was, because if she allowed herself to depend on someone else, if she allowed him to take care of her, she'd use him as an excuse to fall apart.

She swallowed down the useless feelings threatening to consume her. "She's my mom."

"I know." Tony watched her from the other side of the room.

"We'll find her. She'll be okay. Just hang in there a little longer, until we can get a plan together. It's no use going off half-cocked, running on fear."

Twenty minutes later, Tony sequestered his parents in the kitchen with strict orders not to move. Kage, Garrett, and Lance joined Tony and Rocki in the living room. The body shop team opened laptops on the coffee table, made phone calls, and discussed the next plan in quick succession.

She half listened as she filled another magazine clip and stuck Tony's pistol into the back of her jeans. She'd find her mother, even if she had to hunt Marcelli down herself.

"Without knowing who works the other side for Marcelli, it'll be tough to find out where he's hiding." Garrett tapped the keys on the laptop. "Are there others on the force who would help him do his dirty work?"

"I don't…" She cupped her elbows in her hands. "No. I wouldn't think anyone would help him, but I honestly don't know anymore."

The security and trust she always felt while working with some of the best officers in the state was missing this morning. She rubbed her arms, chilled. Who was she supposed to trust?

Soon, every person—from the public to the secretaries to the police chief—would question her integrity. Her defensiveness regarding the situation would label her a troublemaker. She'd heard the warnings for years. Law enforcement officials stayed clean and backed one another. She was not only bringing down one high-profile person within the department, but maybe others before the case closed.

Lance hooked a USB wire from his cell phone to Garrett's laptop. "There were no passengers who purchased tickets last night or this morning who flew out of the Bay City airport between four a.m. and now. Thankfully, BCA is not a normal flight path, and there was only one plane scheduled to leave during that time, headed toward Los Angeles. Again, no walk-on passengers. We're checking the Portland airport now."

The front door crashed open. Rocki jolted, going for her gun. Out of her peripheral vision, all the boys lunged to their feet, brandishing their weapons.

A ticked-off Janie stood in the doorway. "Kage Archer. How dare you leave me at the garage when Rocki needs me?"

Sabrina pushed passed Janie and marched straight toward Garrett. "Yeah. What were you thinking? When a girl's mother is kidnapped, that girl needs her girlfriends, not a bunch of hotheaded boys who won't think of how she's holding up."

Garrett holstered his pistol. "How the hell did you know where we were?"

"I picked the lock at headquarters, shut off the alarm before you'd get a call, and hacked into the main computer to pull up the last recorded phone call you received." Sabrina rocked forward on her toes. "You can yell at me later. Right now, Rocki needs us."

Garrett stalked toward the door. "I swear, I'm going to—"

"Wait." Rocki inhaled, closing her eyes briefly. "As much as I appreciate you two coming to help me, can we concentrate on the situation? Please? This is my mother."

"Kitchen, girls." Tony held his arm out and motioned with his head. "Keep my parents company for a few minutes. Then you can talk with Rocki."

Janie squeezed Rocki's hand. Sabrina kissed her cheek. She nodded at them, touched by their concern. When they were out of the room, she sank down on the arm of the couch.

Lance cleared his throat. "Any other suggestions?"

"We're walking into this blind." Tony stared down at the floor. "Who do we have as an informant that we can use? Think of those we brought in during the last six months on drug charges, and posted bail."

"Gene Baker. Maybe Slim…What's his real name? Steve?" Kage leaned forward. "A better choice would be to go directly to the one who knows everything."

"Who?" Rocki gazed between Kage and Tony. "Whoever it is, I'm in. Let's make contact. We're running out of time."

"No…" Tony ran his hand through his hair. "Not yet. That's our last resort."

She unclutched her arms and walked toward Tony. "Why not?"

"Because I'm talking about going to my uncle," Kage said. "We don't normally deal with him."

"No, that's brilliant!" She fumbled in her pocket for her phone. "I still have his number programmed in my phone. I'll call him now. If anyone knows where Marcelli would hide, it's Darrell."

Tony caught her wrist, stopping her from dialing. "Darrell doesn't do anything without asking for something in return. You're in a safe position. Once he handed the evidence on Marcelli over to you, he wiped his vendetta clean. You're even…His mark on you means nothing if you remain silent. If you ask for his help, you'll owe him, and I won't allow you to put yourself anywhere under his control."

"Tony, it's my mom. I'll deal with Darrell after I get her away from Gino and she's safe. Until then, I'll do whatever it takes to make sure she stays alive." Rocki lifted her chin. "This is one thing I won't let you talk me out of doing."

His mouth tightened and he stared at her. She glared in return. Just because she'd slept with him didn't give him the right to run the search for her mom. She called the shots.

Kage stood. "I'll do it."

"What?" Tony swiveled his gaze to Kage. "I can't believe you'd—"

"Rocki's your woman. I'd do it for Janie…no difference." Kage walked to the front window, putting his back to the room, and used his phone.

"Fucking hell," Tony mumbled. "I owe you. Don't forget it."

Kage shook his head, completely ignoring Tony. Rocki leaned toward Tony and asked, "Do you think Darrell will tell him?"

"Do not talk," he said.

"Tony, you have to—"

"Rocki, so help me, if you don't give me a minute…" He gripped her shoulders. "You have no idea what Kage is doing for me. Not for you, not for himself, but for me."

"I don't understand," she said.

Tony tightened his hold on her. "I know, but trust me. Kage doesn't involve himself in his uncle's business. At all. Ever."

"What's going to happen?"

"He'll owe Darrell. At what price, though… I have no idea." Tony dropped his hands.

She caught his sleeve and stopped him from walking away. "I'll pay him back. I swear. I'll talk to Darrell and transfer the debt off Kage to me."

Tony heaved a sigh and hooked her neck, pulling her closer. "We'll figure this all out, don't worry."

She'd pay anything to have her mother at her side right now. She curved her body against Tony, letting him hold her. Even when she'd worked undercover for Darrell, she'd never been so scared. Without her mom… God, she couldn't even think about that outcome.

Kage turned around. "Got a hit. Marcelli's at the old Sears building a block from the wharf. Two men and a woman have been spotted with him."

Yes. Excitement fueled her forward. She had no say in Tony and Kage going with her, nor did she want to stop long enough to argue with them. The sooner they reached Gino, the faster she could get her mom and keep her safe.

"Wait." Kage stepped in front of Rocki, blocking her from leaving the house.

Her whole body flinched. "What?"

Kage motioned for Tony to come to him, and his gaze softened while he took a deep breath. "There have been reports of gunfire."

She pressed against Tony's arm around her waist, reeling from the news. This was all her fault.

Chapter Twenty-Two

Rocki pressed her back flat to the tin siding of the abandoned Sears building. An old warehouse, two stories tall and long abandoned in the industrial part of town, the building provided minimal coverage with one entrance door facing the street, one exit door at the back of the building, and four delivery doors that were useless to them. She raised the pistol to her chest and gazed at Tony opposite her beside the closed door. She was in no shape to be the first one to kick her way inside the building.

She'd practiced, planned, and gone through every possible scenario that could happen today on the ride over. Her hands shook, despite going through every step of calming herself that she'd learned while on the job. Nothing worked to push the fact that it was her mom inside, and her life was in danger.

The woman who'd raised her singlehandedly and gave her confidence to dream, wish, and not take life too seriously was in the hands of a killer. Her mom had showed her how to keep going and to ignore those who told her that becoming a police detective was impossible for a woman. Mom had supported her when she'd entered the academy, despite her fear that something could happen to her in the line of duty. She readjusted her grip on the gun. Until she saw with her own eyes that Mary was all right, she couldn't trust herself to stay focused on the situation.

Tony motioned from his position on the other side of the entrance. She nodded, but instead of kicking in the door, he stayed in position and studied her.

"Don't go there," he whispered. "Stick with the plan. Get your head straight."

"I know what I'm doing, Weston," she hissed.

He smiled that lopsided grin she loved. "That's my girl. On the count of three."

As instructed, she held up three fingers, two fingers, and then one finger. Tony stepped away from the building and in seconds, he barged forward. She followed Tony as he broke through the door with his shoulder.

They separated, with her going to the right, Tony to the left. She held the gun in front of her, scouring the area.

An old warehouse, barren except for wooden crates left behind years ago, most of them busted by vandals, that dotted the concrete floor. The high windows, covered in dust and grime, blocked the brightest light and she blinked to accustom herself to the dim lighting. She moved forward, scanning the large room.

Toward the west end of the opened floor building, a motorized cart blocked her view. She sidestepped into position, clearing the structure, and spotted her nightmare. She bit off her gasp, steeling herself. Tony moved in front of her the second her gaze landed on her mom.

Around his arm, she viewed Mary sitting on a chair, hands tied behind her, and her mouth moving in surprise at seeing Rocki. Through the rush of her pulse pounding in her ears, she heard her mother speak but couldn't decipher the words. She pushed away the panic and pulled every bit of strength from her resolve. She'd handled situations worse than this before. She knew what to do.

Rocki moved to the left of Tony, staying behind him to make herself less of a target but allowing both of them to have clear shots in case she needed to shoot her way out. She ignored her mom's rustling and concentrated on Marcelli.

Marcelli stood ten feet away from her mother, leaning against a crate, his arms folded and acting as if they'd run into each other at the mall instead of an abandoned warehouse after having just kidnapped her mother. She clenched her teeth together, disgusted and sickened by the truth. Until now, she'd hoped Gino had a fricking good reason to turn his back on the department. What she saw on his face and in the situation told her things were worse than all the proof she had on the detective.

He was a sick bastard who would kill without any thought, and cocky enough to throw the truth in her face and take her down with him.

"It took you an hour longer to find me than I thought it would, Bangli. I taught you better than that." Marcelli tilted his head, letting his hands fall to his sides.

She took in the other two men in the area. Their profiles unfamiliar, she gave them the once-over. Both of them right-handed, and holding a pistol aimed at her and Tony, finger on the trigger. A bulkiness on their right ankles confirmed they were each packing more than one weapon. These guys weren't messing around.

"You have a warrant out for your arrest," she said. "Everyone in the state is looking for you."

"Doesn't matter. Thanks to you, my name means nothing anymore. You've succeeded in killing off Detective Gino Marcelli and making him disappear all by yourself. Unfortunately, I fear you've brought more trouble down on your own head. Without me, the case remains open. You'll never make top detective...such a shame. All that work for nothing." Marcelli pushed away from the crate and walked toward her mom. "Once we're done here, I'll be long gone and you'll be busy cleaning up the mess you created, or not."

Anger rose to the surface, and she forced herself not to show him how much his closeness to her mother bothered her. "And you decided for shits and giggles to kidnap my mom? What's that about?"

Marcelli sighed and swung around to face her. "Insurance, of course. You'll get your mom back when I'm out of the country. It all depends on what you decide to do, Bangli."

"You know I can't let that happen." She stepped forward, not taking her aim off Gino. "I won't let you take her from me, and I'm not letting you slip away."

His men moved forward, arms raised, weapons pointed at her. She ignored them and stopped five feet away from Gino. "I'm not playing your game. If you wanted freedom, you would've taken the first flight out of town the moment you got word that you screwed your own ass by playing both sides."

Gino laughed. The sound, victorious and confident, pissed her off. "Maybe you did learn something working under me."

She widened her stance and waited. Having partnered with Gino many times in the past, taken his tutelage, and mastered his negotiation skills, she knew he wasn't finished. The big finale was coming.

He had a different game plan. One she never suspected. He was out for revenge.

She assumed he'd try to upset her or get her riled, so she lost her head. But he'd shown his real reason why she was standing here talking with him. He wanted her to know what he'd done and throw it in her face. He was proud of going this long without anyone catching on, but he underestimated her. She glanced at Gino's hand.

Sure enough, his finger went to war, trying to rub the prints off his thumb.

"Mom?" She remained looking at Gino. "Are you okay?"

"Yes, honey," Mary said. "Thank you for coming for me. I don't know what we're doing here, but after the way that man pushed me in the car, I knew it had to do with you. I thought your troubles were over."

"Not yet." She paused. "I have a few more things to handle, and then I'll be done."

"Good." Her mom's exhale came out harsh and fast, and Rocki knew her mother understood what was happening. "I took pictures in Hawaii on my phone. I had the loveliest time. The weather was fantastic, and I even lay out on the beach and got a little color on my face. See?"

Rocki wanted to roll her eyes. Only her mom would bring up her getaway-to-stay-safe as a distraction for Rocki.

"That's great. As soon as we're done here, I'll look at your pictures." She moved closer to Tony. "How are you doing, Weston?"

"I'd be better if there weren't three guns aimed at you," he mumbled. "I think it's time to bring this meeting to a close."

"I was thinking the same thing." She walked purposely to Gino. "Call off your thugs."

"Not happening," Gino said. "Bring the evidence you have against me, and I'll let your mom go."

"That's it?" She laughed. "Oh, come on, *Detective* Marcelli. I'm sure you have men inside the department who've already retrieved the package out of the evidence room."

He glared but remained silent.

Bingo.

She'd covered her tracks making sure to double record the evidence, and Marcelli must have found out his moles were unable to

attain the proof. She let herself smile. With what the police department held as evidence, he'd be doing life in prison for what he'd
done.

She walked around him, taking her time, pretending to think
over her next move when really she was checking him out for a
weapon. After making a complete circle, she yawned loudly, irritat-
ing him more as she continued her inspection. On her second trip
around Marcelli, she swung her leg behind his knees, sending him
careening toward the concrete floor.

She wasted no time. In two moves, she had his pistol removed
from his ankle holster and her gun jabbed into the back of his head.
"Tony?"

"Covered." Tony concentrated on the two men in the room.

From her spot beside Gino, she looked across the area. Marcelli's
thugs, distracted by a woman taking down their boss, kept their attention on her and off Tony. "You've got five seconds to hit the door,
or you'll be arrested along with *Mr.* Marcelli."

The men snapped out of their shock, and raised their pistols.
Shots rang out.

She scrambled a few feet and dove for her mom, colliding with
the chair and dragging Mary down underneath her body, shielding
her from getting shot. With her gun hand, she shot the closest man
and took him down with a bullet to his shooting arm. His pistol
flew to the floor ten feet behind him.

Tony clipped the other guy in the thigh, but he remained on his
feet. She saw the injured man move and yelled, but the guy scrambled to the gun and got off one more shot. She jerked her gaze to
Tony and watched him fall to his knees. Rocki screamed louder,
turning to pick off the man, but the scumbag made it to the door
and ran out of sight.

Pushing to her feet, she hurried to Tony. He groaned. Her gaze went to his front and relief swept through her. She sat on her ankles. "Oh, thank God."

"Honey?" her mom said.

"Hang on, Mom." She grasped Tony's shirt and pulled each side, popping buttons. The mark on his bulletproof vest was a welcoming sight. She met his eyes. "You're okay."

"No shit." He chuckled, wincing. "Nothing like setting me up to be your distraction, sweetheart. We need to talk about your leadership skills and who calls the shots."

"Rocki?" her mom called again.

"Yeah?" She dragged her gaze off Tony and turned to her mom. Bile rose in her throat. "Frick."

"First rule of combat, Bangli: do not take your eyes off the suspect." Gino motioned with his pistol for her to stand.

"After all you've done, you deserve to spend time in prison." She raised her hands to her sides, and Gino motioned for her to drop the weapon. She laid the gun on the ground, and stepped away from Tony. "We both know what the men in there will do to you when they discover you're a cop. I'm thinking you deserve everything you'll get. I thought you were one of us, Marcelli. One of the good guys. But you had us all fooled, didn't you?"

"Not happening. I won't be locked up." Marcelli motioned her away from Tony. "Now, you've bought yourself a ticket out of the country. You and your mom are going to take a trip with me."

Tony grunted, coughing hard enough to send him back to the floor. She hesitated. He'd have a bruised sternum tomorrow, but once his breath returned and the pain subsided, he'd be okay. She helped her mom out of the chair.

"Honey, can you unwrap my wrist?" Her mom lifted one of her shoulders. "I can't feel a thing in my fingers."

Rocki glared at Gino. "Can I at least rub her hands?"

The trauma her mom continued to go through would take longer to heal than the bruises from having her hands tied behind her back. She lifted her chin. "She's not used to being tied up or seeing her daughter shot at… The least you can do is let me make her more comfortable. She's my mother, dammit."

Gino glanced at Tony on the floor. "Whatever. Make sure you keep her walking toward the door. I'm running out of time. We're leaving."

With her mom leading the way, she followed behind her and almost choked when she saw the reason why her mom wanted the rope off her wrists. Her mom held a pistol behind her back in her tied hands. She glanced behind her at Gino. He jabbed her in the shoulder with the end of his gun, but hadn't noticed what Mary was holding. Rocki stumbled forward, overexaggerating the push, and took the pistol from her mom.

In one move, she whirled around and aimed the gun at Gino's chest. "Don't move, you bastard."

He cocked his head, and kept his own gun pointed at her. "Looks like a standoff, Bangli."

Another pistol cocked and Tony popped up behind Gino's shoulder. "Let's even the odds. You see, you fucked with my girl, so I don't think I'll wait to see who takes the first shot, because as far as I can see, just your aiming at Rocki is enough for me to kill you. Not to mention kidnapping my girl's mother."

"Shit." Marcelli closed his eyes and lowered the pistol.

Mary nudged her shoulder. "Tony really is sexy, isn't he? Did you hear how he stood up for you… his woman?"

Rocki stepped forward and removed Gino's weapon. As Tony handcuffed Gino, she undid the rope binding her mom's arms.

"How in the world did you end up with a gun when your hands were tied?" Rocki asked.

"Well, when Tony got shot—by the way, I'm glad he was wearing one of those vests—the man who ran out dropped his gun. I got up from the chair, sat down on the floor, rolled over to the gun, and picked it up." Her mom smiled.

"Seriously?" Rocki shook her head. "How did you stand back up and get in the chair without using your hands?"

"Ever since you had me take that self-defense class, I decided I live a pretty sedentary life. I thought I'd change things up and be more active…daring, in the hopes of making myself more agile and limber. So I've been watching YYY DVDs."

Rocki coughed to cover her laugh. "Please don't tell me you meant a triple X DVD."

"Well, that wouldn't make sense when it's called *You, Yoga, and Your Health*. Apparently, it's working, don't you think?" Her mom rubbed her hands together.

Rocki crushed Mary to her chest. "I love you, Mom."

"I love you too, honey." Mary shivered and looked over Rocki's shoulder. "Is this the man you were working undercover with?"

"No, it's someone different. No one important," she said.

"That's good." Her mom leaned closer. "I think he's in a lot of trouble, isn't he?"

"You could say that." She studied Tony. He'd recovered nicely, but she could see the fury etched around his eyes, the pain he ignored, the seriousness of the situation. When he was down on the floor, she'd had a moment of freak-out.

She couldn't lose him. But life with her would bring danger home. She'd already put her mom at risk, and she couldn't ask Tony to handle the consequences of being romantically involved with a detective. He'd already used his parents to help keep her mom safe. What would happen if her life touched him in a negative way? It'd kill everything developing between them.

Tony shoved his phone in his pocket after calling the situation in and pushed Marcelli in front of him, leading the way to the door. She soaked in his control and professionalism. She couldn't believe the situation was finally under control. Not only was her mom's safety her main concern, so was Tony's. Disgust for Gino burned inside of her, and she straightened her shoulders. Whether the bad guy wore blue or was just another drug dealer off the streets, she was proud of making her city a little safer for everyone.

She wanted to tell Tony what she was thinking, and how much she loved him. When she thought him shot, the fear of losing everything they had together pained her worse than if she'd been shot herself. She wanted to tell him how much she loved his support of her career and respected her decisions. He protected her and kept her safe. Not because he believed she needed his help, but because she realized she was the most important person in the world to him.

Instead, she said, "Nice save, gorgeous."

"Don't think I've forgotten about you calling me Weston." His gaze went to her ass. "The name's Tony, sweetheart."

She wrapped her arm around her mother and laughed softly. He might not like her habit of calling him by his last name when they were alone, but she was on to him. He'd purposely riled her earlier to make sure she kept her focus.

Although, she almost lost her cool, and he almost lost his life today, they'd saved her mom and brought in the bad guy. She'd done her job.

Outside in the sunlight, she blinked, letting her eyes adjust to the brightness. Garrett, Lance, and Kage pulled up to the curb in a flash of classic vehicles, followed by three squad cars with their lights and sirens going. Rocki hung back with her mom and let Tony put Marcelli in the rear seat of the holding car.

She turned away, wanting to put her relationship with Marcelli behind her, and spotted a black Lexus parked down the block behind a delivery truck. She stiffened, holding her mother's hand.

"Honey?" Mary said. "Is everything okay?"

"Yeah, sure," she mumbled. "It's all over."

She couldn't find the strength to tell her mom the truth. Her dealings with Darrell Archer weren't finished. She had a debt to pay and had to keep Darrell's name out of the case.

Tony wanted her to stay clear of Kage's uncle, but she was a detective. It was her job to take out the bad guys. As long as the case continued against Gino, she'd be thrust into Darrell's world, despite Tony's advice to run far, far away.

Maybe the best thing to do was walk away from Tony before someone got hurt because of her.

Chapter Twenty-Three

At the request of the Cannon Police Department, the courtroom remained closed to the general public. Only the press, witnesses, and those directly related to the case were given permission inside of the courtroom. That included every off-duty officer from Cannon and Bay City, and a dozen officers from the county sheriff's department.

Rocki stood from the stand and walked back to her seat after Marcelli's attorney drilled her with questions. Her stomach knotted and she forced her shoulders back and her chin up. Seated beside Tony, she allowed herself to inhale a deep breath when he laid his hand on her thigh. The steely warmth from everyone studying her heated her back.

To the others in the room, Tony showed his support silently and unconditionally. For her, she zoned in on his constant, strong hand as a lifeline. The glares and mistrust she'd viewed from the other officers sitting behind her cut to the bone. They were called in as witnesses for the defense. Marcelli's ties went deep in the department.

Wearing a shield meant she'd dedicated her life to the force. She'd sworn to protect not only innocent citizens, but also every one of the officers sitting in the room decked out in their dress uniform. What they didn't understand fully was she was protecting them by bringing the evidence forward.

In time, she hoped they'd understand she did the right thing, the expected thing. The only thing her heart would allow her to do.

Once they grasped the seriousness of what Marcelli had done, they'd come to accept her actions for what they were. She'd cleaned the streets of yet another drug dealer and murderer.

The judge cleared his throat. "We'll recess for one hour."

Tony leaned toward her and whispered, "I need to find Kage."

"Okay." She stood, holding his hand. "I'll go with you."

Tony's concern over Kage touched her. She'd tried talking to him before, many times, but the topic of Kage was off-limits. His worry about Darrell coming after Kage remained heavy on Tony's mind. Although Darrell had seemingly gone underground after she'd captured Marcelli, because no one had seen him.

Ignoring the others in the courtroom, she left through the back door. Tony led her to his Camaro. She glanced at him while buckling her seat belt.

He'd stayed quiet all morning, worrying that the details of the case would come out before he had the chance to talk to Kage. A high-profile media frenzy would speculate and announce the verdict the moment the recess ended, and they couldn't guarantee the death of Kage's mom by Marcelli wouldn't be leaked.

Three blocks away, they pulled into the parking lot of an apartment building and Rocki took in the area. She'd been called there plenty of times while on duty. It was known for housing illegals, drug dealers, and a more unsavory crowd, and every officer from Cannon knew the place personally. She exited the car and met Tony in front of the vehicle. He threw his arm around her shoulders.

"Stick close," he muttered.

"Is there a reason Lance lives here?" she asked. "I mean, he's got a good job. Not that he can't live wherever he wants, I'd just think he'd want to…I don't know, be safe."

"His grandmother, a very proud Irish woman, owns the building and refuses to move. Lance stays close to his granny to make sure she's protected and safe. His reputation is well known here as someone people don't want to mess with." Tony climbed the steps without letting her go. "He does as much as he can to keep out with the troublemakers, but his grandmother believes everyone deserves to have a roof over their head and the right to live somewhere they can call home…so he watches out for Granny McCray."

Okay, her respect for Lance rose to a megalevel. His granny. The guys from Beaumont Body Shop never failed to amaze her.

Tony knocked on the door. "Yo," he called.

At the return answer, Tony opened the door. She followed him inside. Janie, Sabrina, and, to her surprise, Charlene swept her up into a cluster hug. She squeezed her eyes closed as their arms surrounded her from all sides and pulled her away from Tony. Their unexpected support hit her hard. Until she'd walked inside, she had no idea she'd been holding herself tense and putting up a front.

She laid her head on someone's shoulder—Sabrina's, if she went by the faint whiff of jasmine. Her throat tightened and words of thanks got caught in her mouth. All she could do was hold on and let them help relieve some of the pressure she was under.

Eventually, she straightened and pulled herself together. Janie swept her finger under each of Rocki's eyes. Lighter for their show of friendship, she inhaled deeply. She moved her mouth, not knowing if she was thanking them or babbling like an idiot, but they told her she was welcome.

"Enough of the drama," Charlene said. "We need tequila to put a smile on everyone's faces again."

She shook her head. "I can't. We need to get back to the court-house soon. I'll be so glad when the trial is over and behind me. The others"—she swallowed—"God, they hate me."

"Screw them." Janie grabbed her shoulders and faced her. "You're doing the right thing. Good always trumps bad. Remember that."

She nodded. "I need to use the bathroom to wash my face before we head back."

"I'll show you were it is." Janie pulled her through the apartment and walked her to the bathroom.

She closed the door, went about her business, and when she was done, she washed her face before exiting the room. Janie stood with her arms crossed, watching her. The overbearing-best-friend act should've humored her, but for some reason Janie made her feel guilty. Yet it felt natural and she was hit again with how close she and Janie had grown since that awful meeting when she'd returned Bluff after Darrell stole Janie's cat for leverage.

"He'll be okay," Janie said.

"What?" She swiped the back of her hand across her cheek.

"Tony. He's a good guy, and I've known him my whole life. I can tell when something's bothering him."

She leaned her hip against the door frame. "I don't know what to do for him."

"You're doing it. Whatever is going on inside his head has noth-ing to do with you. He watches you. Not like a man who doesn't know where he stands, but like a man who is in love," Janie said. "He'll work through it."

She nodded. "Yeah."

He was in love with her? Rocki set the towel on the counter. Her heart raced. He hadn't said the words, but he'd shown her how much she meant to him time and time again. He'd tattooed a picture of her on his arm. She reached out and squeezed Janie's hand. "Will you make sure he stays okay?"

Janie stiffened. "Me?"

"Yeah." She peered down the hallway and lowered her voice. "You know, in case things don't work out for Tony and me. My life...I'm a detective. Tony was shot because of me, my mom was kidnapped, and Tony's parents got involved just to keep my mother safe. I can't have my job hurting Tony or the people he loves, because he's involved with me."

"Bitch," Janie whispered. "You're leaving him."

She steeled her back. "I have a career."

"So does Tony." Janie clamped her lips together. "I thought you were the one."

Several seconds ticked by, and Rocki said, "So did I."

She returned to the living room and found Tony watching her intently. She smiled, knowing he worried about her. She'd be okay.

Later, she'd explain to him the emotional drama girls could have when situations got too tough. Not that she'd experienced many meltdowns in her lifetime, until meeting Tony and the others. Now tears came often for the craziest reasons, some of them warranted.

At Tony's side, she leaned against him and put her hand on his stomach. She took the time to look around Lance's place. The inside of the apartment belied the rough exterior.

The walls were a rich cream color, except for the dark maroon-painted wall behind the dartboard that entertained Garrett and Lance. The accent worked with the throw pillows on the couch and the rug covering the hardwood floors. Tastefully decorated. She wondered if Lance had a girlfriend and why she'd never met her during all the times they'd gotten together to hash out the case.

Garrett shoved Lance away from the board on the other side of the room in a friendly competition. Kage reclined on the couch with Janie now on his lap. Rocki warmed. Seeing those two together gave her confidence that she and Tony could work something out between them.

A private investigator and a detective would always butt heads, but they were good together. She trusted him and though he never said it, he showed her it was okay to lean on him for support without him judging her. That devotion would get him in trouble. She pressed tighter against Tony.

She loved him.

Not once had she met a man who put everyone else first in his life and could still take time for himself. He loved his dog, his friends, and his family, which told her everything she needed to know. The respect for the guys, the creativity he put into the cars he built from scrap into showroom classics, and the ability to show her how much he cared for her made him the perfect man. It didn't hurt that he had the most beautiful smile that took her breath away, and that smile came often and easily.

"Have you decided whether you're going to see Darrell like he requested?" Tony asked Kage.

Kage watched the game going on across the room, not facing Tony. Rocki wondered if he was even aware of Tony speaking to him, except for the slight chin dip Kage gave and the softening of Tony's body.

"All right. Good. We'll go directly to the garage after court gets out." Tony swiped a throw pillow off the couch, and tossed it at Garrett who was in mid-aim. "We're taking off. We'll see you back at Body Shop after the trial. Be there."

The room quieted, and all eyes seemed to land on Rocki. The lump in her throat returned full force, and she buried her face in Tony's neck and mumbled.

Tony's chest rumbled beneath her cheek. "I think she's saying thank you."

She talked against his skin again.

"And she'd like pizza tonight…" he said.

Rocki laughed on a sob, playfully slapping his chest. "I said, I can't believe how much they mean to me."

Tony kissed her forehead. "Yeah, that too. The pizza was my idea. I'm starved."

Everyone moved at once, and before she could talk individually to the ones who encouraged her not to give up, she was outside, sucking in air, hoping she didn't ruin her makeup with all the encouragement she received from her new friends.

When they pulled into the courthouse parking lot ten minutes later, Tony turned off the engine of the Camaro. "Ready?"

"Yeah. No." She remained seated, not even undoing her seat belt. "What's up with Kage?"

Tony leaned back and sighed. "His uncle contacted him and asked for a meeting today, after the court hearing."

"Is he going to go?"

He nodded. "Yep. He acts as if nothing is wrong, but I know him. He has no idea what Darrell's done all these years. I'm worried about how he'll take the news once he finds out the truth. I don't want him doing something stupid, or he'll regret it for the rest of his life."

"You care about him," she whispered.

They were men, but their friendship was tight. Tighter than any relationship she'd ever seen. They stood beside each other through thick and thin, and supported each other unconditionally.

"Yeah." He leaned over and kissed her hard. "Let's go, sweetheart."

"Wait." She held his hand. "We need to talk."

He tilted his head. "'Kay."

If she had more time and they weren't obligated to walk into the courtroom, she'd discuss why she'd come to the decision to break things off with him now, rather than later. He was too good of a guy to hit below the belt, in a car, when she needed more time to explain her decisions. But she didn't have time.

"A lot has happened—"

"I know that, sweetheart," he said.

She nodded. "I'm a detective. This is only one case, but there will be many more. Some easier, some more dangerous."

"Right," he said, leaning back against the seat. "What are you saying?"

She took in the hardness of his mouth, the intensity of his gaze, and wanted to change her mind. She'd known from the beginning that circumstances threw them together and with all the drama in their lives, they ran off pure emotion. They went from needy to hot in a matter of days, and yet acted as if they'd been together years.

Personally, she clung to him. Her defenses were down, and he'd met her at her most vulnerable. That state of mind allowed her to be herself and let him inside her head. She loved every minute having him in her life.

"After this is all over with, I'm going to have to move back with my mom, pick up another case, and, I don't know…it might be another undercover job. I could be gone for a while." She glanced away. "I think we should take a break—"

"Fuck that," he said. "You can work. You can even go undercover, because that's your job. But if you think you're walking away from me because you're saving me from a life of having your smile, your laughter, your hands on my body, then you're whacked. Sweetheart, I wanted you for almost a year. I never approached you, because you were a woman who wouldn't settle for a man who'd give you anything less than everything. I stayed away from you because I thought

I wasn't ready for something real. Now I know you, and I know there's no one else I want. Ever. It's more than wanting you. I *need* you in my life every day. If that means I have to go weeks or months without you, because of your career, then knowing you're mine and you'll come back to me is all I need."

"I deal with bad people every day. Look what happened to you, my mom—"

"Your mom is fine. I'm good." He leaned closer. "Got it?"

She shook her head. "I won't—"

He kissed the end of her nose. "I'm not going anywhere, and I'm sure as hell not letting you leave me."

"I don't want you to blame me if something goes wrong," she whispered. "What happens if danger comes to you or your parents because of me?"

"That's what I'm here for." He waited until she gazed up at him again, and then he continued. "Let me take care of you. Save your strength for your cases. I have all the confidence that on the job you can take care of yourself. I won't let anything happen to anyone in our lives, especially you."

"But what if something *does* happen?" She swallowed hard. "What if I can't control a situation and someone follows me home, or a person comes after you to get to me?"

"Then we deal with it." He smiled and softened his voice. "Together, we make a hell of a team."

She stared into his eyes, swallowed past her doubts, and softened. "Yeah."

"Yeah." He chuckled. "We'll talk later. Right now, you need to go into the courtroom and see that justice prevails."

Before she was ready to let the subject drop, they were inside the courtroom, and the room was called to order. The jury returned to its spot off to the side of the judge's desk. She stood as the bailiff called attention to stand, and Judge Chedwich took the bench.

Stout, unemotional, and keeping his gaze on the platform in front of him, Judge Chedwich gave those waiting in the courtroom no hint of what the verdict would be. Rocki sat down, thankful for the hard seat below her butt. She barely had enough oxygen in her body to support standing up without getting dizzy.

Her career was on the line. If Marcelli walked, she could kiss her chance of ever being top detective and fitting in with the others in the department good-bye. She'd have to find a job in a different jurisdiction, a different district, and still she worried that her reputation of going against one of her own would follow her. A shield doesn't convict another shield.

Unable to restrain her curiosity over whether Marcelli was showing signs of worry, Rocki gazed to the left. Marcelli sat at attention in his chair beside his lawyer, his eyes straight ahead, no expression on his face, and confident as can be. Her gaze lowered. On top of the table, his folded hands rested, except for his thumb and finger constantly moving.

He might be able to fool others, but she knew him well. He was nervous and he couldn't hide that fact from her.

Behind him sat his wife, Susan. Rocki bit the inside of her lip. She liked Marcelli's wife. On several occasions, she'd talked with Susan during the backyard barbecues at the Marcelli house when the squad got together during the summer. A quiet woman who played a gracious hostess didn't deserve having her life destroyed and her reputation shredded for what her husband had done.

Susan turned and caught her eye. Rocki swallowed at the intensity in the other woman's gaze. What was Susan thinking while watching and hearing what the accusations were against her husband? What Rocki had accused Marcelli of doing?

Susan lowered her gaze, and their connection was gone. But right before Marcelli's wife turned away, she'd seen what she was searching for to ease her mind. Acceptance.

Somewhere in the back of Susan's thinking, she knew the other woman held no ill will toward Rocki. Maybe she'd known what her husband was doing or she believed the accusations were true. Whatever thought process it took to understand that your husband could be going away for life, Susan would survive the jury's decision.

The judge finished his rehearsed speech and the first juror stood. Rocki grabbed Tony's hand and kept her gaze to the front. Her heart pounded so hard, the speaker's words blurred together. Nevertheless, she caught the first ruling.

"On one charge of kidnapping, we find Gino Marcelli...guilty," the female juror said.

She squeezed Tony's hand. At least Marcelli would go down for messing with her mom.

On and on for five minutes, the charges against her former supervisor and friend came in. All charges, except one for witness tampering, brought him a guilty verdict. At the outburst from the room, the judge brought order to the court while Gino's attorney stood and tried speaking over the crowd.

Tony stood and ushered her toward the center aisle. She stepped around the last chair. Her gaze met Gino's as two armed guards brought him to his feet and handcuffed him for transportation to Oregon State Penitentiary. She schooled her features, pivoted, and walked out of the room with her head held high. It was over.

Several of her commanding officers, other detectives, and police officers shook her hand on the way to the double doors in the back of the room. She murmured appropriate responses and stayed by Tony's side.

There would be no celebrating in view of the others. No smile of victory. Regardless of her elation, one of their own went down today.

Inside, she knew she'd put a bad guy away, taken one dealer off the street. She called that a good day, because good always trumps bad.

Chapter Twenty-Four

Tony pulled into the parking lot of Beaumont Body Shop trailed by a black Lexus. His gaze went to the garage. Kage's Mustang, Lance's Harley, Garrett's Barracuda were already parked outside the garage, having arrived before them.

"Sweetheart, hold the steering wheel." He slowed down and when Rocki guided the car straight head, he reached behind him, under the seat, and removed his pistol he'd hidden there while they were in the federal building earlier. "Okay. Grab the clip out of the glove box for me."

Once he had everything, he loaded the gun, set it between his legs, and parked. "If I asked you to stay in the car, would you?"

"Um, not in this lifetime." She disconnected her seat belt. "Whatever Darrell's up to, I want to be there. I owe Kage for all he's done for me, and if there's an opportunity to nail Darrell, I'll take it."

"Kage can handle his uncle. He's been on his own his whole life and has kept himself away from having anything to do with Darrell." Tony squeezed her hand.

"What?" Her brows wrinkled. "I was under the impression, going from the paperwork the department has collected over the years, the Archer's were a close, albeit dysfunctional family."

He sighed. "His dad's in prison, sweetheart. His mom, as you know, is dead. Kage has managed to stay out of his uncle's business this long, and he won't go back. I'd say he's strong enough to handle anything Darrell throws at him."

"But he doesn't know—"

"No. He doesn't." Tony opened his door, but before he stepped out he said, "And when he does find out, it's going to knock him on his ass."

Darrell, Kage, Garrett, Lance, Tony, and Rocki congregated in the parking lot as if they'd planned this moment for weeks instead of a few hours ago. Tony stood beside Kage and sent Rocki off to join the girls at the back door to the body shop to help keep an angry Janie from getting any closer to Darrell.

Tony focused on Kage. He wanted to ask if Kage was okay, but he already knew the answer. Whether being this close to Kage's uncle bothered him or not, Kage would never speak of his feelings.

"Your only job is to keep Janie safe," Kage said without taking his gaze off his uncle.

Tony slipped his pistol in the back of his jeans and nonchalantly hooked the thumb of his nonshooting hand in his front pocket. "That's a given, bro. Always."

Garrett flanked Kage's other side. "What's your uncle want this time?"

"Same shit, same drug lord," Kage murmured.

Tony knew why Darrell called the visit. Tightness crawled up his neck. He just didn't know whether Kage's uncle would share the truth after all these years or create another lie to fuck with Kage's head. He studied Darrell as he approached the group, staying ten feet away.

Polished in a black suit, cream-colored shirt, and navy tie, Darrell appeared in total control. Tony scanned the area. Darrell never went anywhere without his thugs, yet not one of them was in sight.

"Kage." Darrell unbuttoned his suit coat.

Kage refused to acknowledge him. Tony stared straight ahead, all his attention toward the front in case any of Darrell's men decided to show their faces. Kage's lack of emotion over the family meeting was normal and what Tony expected from his friend. He had more self-control than a man had a right to own.

Darrell studied the area beyond them. Tony's gaze followed in the same direction, and his stomach tightened. Rocki stood in front of Janie, glaring at Darrell.

"I hear congratulations are in order, Detective Bangli." Darrell dipped his chin. "Our deal has been finalized to a mutual satisfaction, I believe."

Rocki's brows lifted. Tony shifted. He'd seen that look on her face before. Now was not the time to rile Darrell. She was free, and he'd like to keep her that way.

"You do know I won't give up on taking you down," Rocki said. "It's my job."

Oh, fuck. Tony reached behind him, gripped his gun, and waited.

Darrell chuckled. "I wouldn't expect anything less from you, Detective. You'll keep me on my toes and I'll keep you entertained, I'm sure. I look forward to seeing you again."

"Don't even think about it," Tony said. "She's mine."

Darrell's jaw twitched and he swung his gaze back to the group of men. "I'll take that into consideration, Weston."

"Nobody calls him Weston," Rocki said.

He turned in time to watch Janie hold Rocki from going after Darrell. He nailed her with a look, and inhaled deeply when Rocki stepped back beside the other women heeding his silent plea to back off. A fierce pride came from her standing up to Darrell. No matter how foolish or useless the stance was, he knew where she stood.

"You've got thirty seconds to say what you came here to say, and then I'm going inside and you're getting in your fucking car and leaving," Kage said.

During the whole exchange Kage stood patiently waiting, but he'd put an end to the game Darrell wanted. Kage's hands relaxed at his sides, his face a mix of boredom and disinterest in what was happening around him. Tony clenched his teeth. He should've told Kage when he and Rocki made the deal and broken his promise to Kage's uncle.

He owed Kage.

"They'll be some news that comes out in the press regarding Gino Marcelli that directly involves you." Darrell took one step forward. "I wanted you to hear it from me first."

"Nothing that involves you would surprise me, or the fact that I would get dragged into the mess," Kage said. "Save your breath."

Darrell tilted his head and studied Kage. "You've always had a strength I admired. You do know that, don't you, Kage?"

Kage remained silent.

"Very well." Darrell clasped his hands behind his back. "Your friend Wes—Tony has already been informed of the details, and I can see that he too has kept his word. You've accomplished a lot with such loyal friends. Some say to have friends, you don't need money. I've found that untrue but like always, you've taken a different approach than I, or your father."

"Bastard," Tony whispered.

Whether Darrell drew out the truth to nail them all or to cause Kage more pain, Tony wanted the meeting over and done. He stepped forward, but Darrell put up his hand stopping him.

"The shipment of heroin your mother was testing all those years ago came from Marcelli, and wasn't part of my stock." Darrell lowered his voice. "Marcelli was the one who killed your mother, Kage. The batch wasn't mine. What you witnessed was me trying to help your mother after she'd injected the heroin to test it during a buyout."

Tony expected Kage to lurch forward, to go after his uncle, to reel back in shock, or to stare dumbfounded at the news. Instead, Kage took the information as if Darrell had announced the chrome bumper on Kage's Mustang had a dirty spot.

Garrett cussed. "Is that true?"

"Yeah." Tony swallowed. "He handed proof to Rocki and in return she presented evidence in court supporting the fact. They pinned the death of not only Kage's mom, but also five others on Marcelli. I gave my word to Darrell during his meeting with Rocki and me that I wouldn't tell Kage in exchange for keeping Rocki safe until she could bring in Marcelli."

And still, Kage stood there unaffected by the news.

Darrell pulled his lips tight against his teeth. A crack in his armor. He gave a damn, but for what reason, Tony would never know. If Darrell thought to weaken Kage's resolve to stay out of the family business, he was sadly mistaken. He knew in his heart, Kage would never walk on the other side of the road and work for the underground.

"We're done," Kage said, pivoting and walking off.

Janie ran to him, but the only sign Kage knew she was there was that his hand went to her hip and he held her against his side.

"Kage," Darrell called.

Kage stopped, but kept his back toward his uncle. Tony walked forward joining Garrett behind Kage. Lance joined them and together the three of them surrounded Kage, shoulder to shoulder, blocking Kage from Darrell's view. It wasn't the first time they'd protected Kage's back, and it wouldn't be the last time. Even though he trusted Kage to stay away from Darrell, he knew Darrell would never give up trying to bring his nephew into the family business. He'd personally stop his friend before he ruined his life.

"While you believed I was the one responsible for you losing your mother, it kept you safe," Darrell said. "It strengthened your resolve to stay out of the underground, away from me, and made you the better man." He paused. "I did it for *you*, Kage. You're blood. You're my family."

Tony sucked in air. *Shit.* He was not expecting that.

Kage raised his hand in acknowledgment, and walked forward toward the back door of the body shop without saying another word in reply to his uncle's confession. Tony followed everyone into the building. He couldn't imagine what Kage was going through.

"We still have a while before it's happy hour at Corner Pocket." Kage headed down the hallway with Janie, leading all of them toward the garage. "Let's cut that sunroof into Garrett's Duster before we go have a beer."

"Sounds good to me. I could use a drink," Garrett said.

Sabrina hurried to catch up with Garrett. "I get to turn on the air compressor."

"I'll sit back and ogle the man candy. I'll even slip you boys a dollar if you leave off the coveralls." Charlene cackled.

Janie leaned her head against Kage's arm, and the sight pleased Tony. Kage had somebody, and he hoped in private, his friend would lean on the woman who loved him. The business with Darrell rocked Kage's foundation of what he'd built his life around, and he'd need his woman. He'd need them all before this was over.

Tony reached out and slipped Rocki's hand inside his. She looked at him and bit her lip, asking him with her eyes whether everything was okay. He shrugged and followed the group. He couldn't explain how they all coped with their connection to Darrell, they just did.

"Beers are on me tonight," he said.

Despite keeping busy and the girls distracting everyone, Tony kept his eyes on Kage throughout the installation of the sunroof. His friend would be all right, he had no doubt. But he worried about how Kage would accept the truth, and he'd wait in case Kage wanted to talk. The news changed the reasoning behind Kage's hatred for his uncle, and who knew what the future would bring him.

For that matter, he had no fucking clue what was going to happen between him and Rocki. Her trying to put distance between them was the last thing he'd expected today. Before he did anything, he wanted to make sure she realized he wasn't letting her go.

Chapter Twenty-Five

Beer in hand, sexy guy's arm looped across her shoulders, Rocki stood beside pool table number three at Corner Pocket's where her life had changed for the better. She held on to the cue stick, leaning against her man. She fought against giggling her pleasure at her propitious turn of events. Tony lost the last game of pool to her, and she was about to clean the table again.

Ecstatic over the win, she'd done her best to keep up the momentum. That included leaning into him tightly and palming his ass with her free hand. He jolted, and she moved in for the kill. She had one more shot, and she needed to win.

"Winner calls," she whispered, nibbling on his neck.

"Right," he said.

She stepped away from him, bent over the table, and glanced behind her. "Anything, gorgeous."

He flashed her one of his killer smiles. "Hell, yeah."

Then she cleared the table of balls. Winning was her name today, and Tony deserved what she had planned for later when they returned to his house.

"Damn. You played me the night we met, acting like you couldn't sink even two balls back to back." Tony whistled. "Remind me to never bet you when we play pool."

She grinned. Life was about to get interesting.

Darrell no longer wanted her silenced, Marcelli was in prison, and the guys at work would eventually realize she'd had their back the whole time. She vibrated with excitement for the future. Her relationship with Tony could go forward.

She believed him when he said they'd work out any problems together. They made an awesome team, and she had all the confidence in the world that if she tried to lead them in the wrong direction, he'd be the voice of reason in the relationship. Not that she wouldn't try to push him into her way of thinking. Trying to change Tony's mind was the fun part.

"You are going to love what I have planned for you," she said, walking into his embrace.

He squeezed her to his chest. She smiled at the hammering of his heart, which she could feel over the music playing in the background. For a split second, she wondered if things were going *too* well.

Relationships usually never worked for her. Friends went to the wayside because of her career. Boyfriends tired of her need to control the relationship. Yet, Tony fit into her life better than if she'd handpicked him herself.

He took away her need for control and let her be herself. He made her feel like the most precious woman in the world. He allowed her to open up and be vulnerable, which was what she needed in her line of work. She had no desire to be the strong fearless detective at home. No, home was where she wanted to be Tony's woman and please her man.

She gazed at Janie sitting on Kage's lap. She'd never had girlfriends who pushed their way into her life and refused to leave the way Janie, Sabrina, and even Charlene had done. They understood her needs without her saying a word. They accepted her without any explanation.

"Honey?" Her mom hurried toward her. "Caleb and Pauline are taking me home before they head to the hotel. Then I'm going to help them find a Realtor tomorrow. They're thinking about moving back to Bay City. Isn't that wonderful?"

Rocki looked at Tony. He pointed to her and grinned. She slapped his arm at the reminder of her lie. She did not sell real estate.

"Did you know your parents wanted to move back?" she asked.

Tony shrugged, but seemed to accept the news. "Nothing surprises me when it comes to my parents. They're retired, and go where they want."

Rocki left Tony's arms and entered her mom's embrace. "That's wonderful. You seem to really like the Westons."

Her mom nodded. "I do. We got to know each other in Hawaii and we have something in common."

"What?" she asked.

"You and Tony." Her mom kissed her cheek before moving to Tony and raising up on her toes to give him a kiss too. "Take care of my baby."

"I will," Tony winked at Rocki.

Caleb stepped forward, shook Tony's hand, and then hugged her. Not any hug, but a hug that spoke more of the depth of the man. He loved his only son and wanted him happy. She understood and squeezed him back, a lump forming in her throat.

Pauline took Caleb's place in front of her. "I'm so happy everything worked out for you."

"Me too." She hugged Pauline. "Thank you for taking care of my mom. I appreciate you being there for her."

"No thanks needed. We were glad to help." Pauline smoothed

Rocki's hair off her shoulder and whispered, "Stick with my boy, sweetie. He's falling in love with you, you know."

She pulled back. "What?"

Pauline smoothed Rocki's cheek with her hand. "He hasn't said anything to me, but a mother knows."

Tony walked his parents and her mom outside. She stood in the same spot, staring at the door. That was the second person who'd claimed to know what Tony was feeling toward her. With the excitement in their life and the trial, she'd ignored the fact that Tony hadn't mentioned love in the equation. Neither had she.

Her whole body squealed in the most wonderful way and she looked around the room, spotted Sabrina, and rushed over to her. She had to tell someone, anyone, to make the moment real. Laughing, she threw herself on Sabrina and forced her to jump up and down with her.

Relief swept through her. "I'm falling in love with Tony."

"Girlfriend, we already knew that." Sabrina planted her hands on her shoulders, stopping the movement. "You're supposed to tell Tony that, not me."

"I will." She inhaled a big breath. "Tonight."

Lance stood from the nearby table, knocking his chair over in the process. "What the hell?"

Rocki turned and found Tony walking toward her with the cutest old lady she'd ever seen. She glanced back at Lance. "Who's that?"

The elderly woman took Lance's attention and he moved in front of Rocki. "Granny McCray, what are you doing here?"

Granny McCray?

No more than five feet tall, curly short gray hair, stooped, and wielding a metal cane, Granny hobbled up to Lance and poked him hard in the belly. "You're needed at home."

Lance looked toward the ceiling. "What now, Granny?"

"Don't give me any lip, boy." Granny's cane flew out in the other direction, almost hitting Tony. "*She* needs your help."

Rocki followed the direction of the cane. A gorgeous woman with long straight black hair stepped out from behind Tony. Rocki whispered, "Wow."

Along with a perfect tight body and kick-ass outfit, the woman sent a glare straight to Lance that screamed she was looking for trouble. Rocki skirted the stare-down between Lance and the woman, and moved to Tony's side.

Tony grabbed her hand. "Let's get out of here while we can."

"Maybe we should stay and see what's wrong," she said.

"Hell, no. I lost a bet playing pool and I'm willing to pay." He laughed as he pushed the door open and strolled outside.

Fifteen minutes later at Tony's house, in the bedroom, Rocki hung on to Tony. She had no time to put her plan into action. He'd gone all business on her in the driveway, half dragging her inside and holding her while he quickly put Brute out for his nighttime potty business.

Hot, hard, aggressive, Tony held up his part of the bargain. He slid his hand underneath her hair and cupped her head as he crashed against the wall, cushioning her to his chest. She melted as his hand covered her lower back, holding her tight. Heat rolled off his body, warming hers.

"Damn." He kissed her again. "Sweetheart, I want you." He palmed her ass. "Now."

"Yes." She wiggled away from him and dragged him to his bedroom.

He picked her up and fell onto the bed with her in his arms, holding her against him. Touching, kissing, stripping his clothes off, she flailed beside him in her rush. "Hurry."

"I'm trying, sweetheart." He ripped out the laces on his boots, pulled them off before he pushed his jeans down and kicked his legs, sending his pants to the floor.

She nibbled across his chest, over the taunt muscles. Her nails dug into his shoulders. Tony laughed as she peered into his face, realizing she'd created a wild man. He'd gone from laughing in the car to pushing the pedal to the metal and breaking all kinds of speeding laws to get her home.

Her heart burst with wonderful feelings, and she wanted to tell him everything. "Tony, I—"

"I know. Me too, sweetheart." Once again, his hand went to her hair. He pushed his fingers through the strands, then dropped his head and touched his lips to her mouth.

She felt his lips on her cheek, her neck, and her hand weaved around his ribs, his waist, drawing him closer. She absorbed every hard angle and plane. The muscles in his back flexed beneath her fingertips. His erection pressed against her.

He sucked on her earlobe, the sound of his breath rasping in her ear. Her eyelids drifted shut. Her heart was at stake here. She could no more leave him than quit the force. He was a part of her now.

His hands moved in front of her, sliding between their bodies. The warmth of his fingers seeped into her skin, and she shivered in delight.

His thumbs brushed her nipples and he whispered, "You're my dream girl."

Okay, she liked that. She smiled.

He skimmed his thumbnail over the hard tip of her breast. She gasped. Jolts of pleasure pinged throughout her body. Desire built, expanded, and demanded more. She stroked him, needing him inside of her.

His breathing grew harsh. She squirmed against him, until he guided her on top of him, and he settled below her. "We're going too fast, sweetheart. I need to slow down."

She sucked her bottom lip between her teeth and clamped down. A moan escaped and she wanted to rush and meet him at the finish line before something happened to stop them. "Fast is good."

He spread his hands on her hips. "Fast is going to kill me."

She blinked, forcing herself to hear past their ragged breaths, past the soft rustle of her knees rubbing against the comforter as she found it impossible to sit still when his warm body sat between her thighs. Beyond them, silence filled the room.

The air sizzled. He ran his palm up the inside of her leg. She couldn't speak at the slow torture of him almost touching, but not quite in the area she wanted him to be.

Even as they positioned themselves, he never stopped watching her. He cupped her, rubbed her, and her breathing grew shallow and rapid. He slid his finger along her wetness. She gasped and braced herself on his chest.

"Don't move," he whispered.

He trailed his finger forward and rubbed. She squeezed her eyes shut. "Oh. My. G—"

"Look at me, sweetheart."

She should've anticipated that he'd control their night. Even winning the pool game, Tony gave her what she asked for, what she'd won. His callused finger slid inside of her. He understood, and he continued pleasuring her, until she shattered into a million pieces.

He stroked her thighs, letting her recover. She blinked away the moisture gathering in her vision. "Tony," she murmured.

"I know." He rolled her over, until he was on top of her, settled between her legs.

He moved slowly at first. She could feel the tension coiled in his shoulders. Inch by inch, he plunged inside until they were fully connected. He hissed. She cupped his face, and arched against him.

She reveled in his shudder. That she brought a man his size, his strength, his determination to a level where he trembled in her arms left her delirious.

"You feel so good." He moved back and forth, sliding, caressing her from the inside out.

She gave a throaty moan as his thrust sped up. His arms shook with the effort it took to restrain himself. She raised her hips, meeting him halfway as her body rejuvenated below him. She needed more. He deserved more. She locked her ankles behind his hips and wrapped her arms around his neck.

She pulled him down, sinking her mouth against the curve of his neck. "Weston…"

He grunted, thrusting fully inside her.

She held on tight as she came. Her whole body constricted. Waves of pleasure pulsated, taking all her strength. Distantly aware of him letting go of his own release, she dropped down onto the mattress.

He remained inside of her, poised above and looking…immensely pleased with himself.

"I love you," he whispered, more intensely than ever.

Her whole body warmed and melted over hearing the words for the first time. "I love you too," she whispered back.

They held each other. Her thoughts went to the excitement of going toward the next step in their relationship. He seemed to be gathering his strength.

Finally, he lifted his head, rolled to the side, taking her with him, and growled in her ear. "You called me Weston."

She laughed.

He pushed himself to his elbow and stared down at her. Finally it hit him. "Shit, woman. You do it on purpose, don't you?"

She sucked in her bottom lip and nodded. "You go all badass in a sexy way I find impossible not to love."

He flopped back on the bed, chuckling. She draped herself across his chest and looked down into his face. "You're going to drive me crazy, Detective Bangli. Nothing but trouble."

She smiled, knowing she couldn't lie. "You haven't seen anything yet, gorgeous."

Don't miss the first book in Debra Kayn's Hard Body series.

Please turn the page for an excerpt from

Archer.

Prologue

Mr. Anderson, Jane's employer, waved over his shoulder and wished her a good night as he pushed through the front doors of the attorney's office. She echoed her own good wishes and removed her purse out of the bottom drawer on her desk before the door stopped swinging. She thought he'd never leave.

Every minute past seven o'clock put her on edge. Scott hated when she came home late, no matter what day it was or how many messages she left on his voice mail informing him she was required to stay at work. She glanced at her watch. Maybe if she took the freeway instead of driving through downtown, her tardiness wouldn't raise Scott's suspicions.

The cool wind swept over her as she locked the door and stepped out from under the awning. She shivered, holding her keys in her hand and hurrying across the parking lot. Her red Duster, a Sweet Sixteen birthday present from her dad many years ago, parked at the end of the lot was the only remaining car left at the miniplex.

The bloodred paint with metallic flakes sparkled from the light of one of the security lamps dotting the area, filling her with warmth and a reminder of home. Her brother, Garrett, surprised her when she graduated college by painting her car and detailing it out. His friend Kage was responsible for the mag wheels that grabbed every man's attention who drove by. She raked her teeth over her bottom lip. Scott hated those wheels. He'd become enraged when he found out Kage gave her a gift that cost over a thousand dollars and had split her lip when he slapped her.

At least she got to keep the tires.

Her car reminded her of everyone she loved. Her dad, Garrett, Kage, and her old friends back in Bay City, Oregon. She'd give anything to return home. Now even that dream was lost to her. Scott had proven he'd find her anywhere she tried to run.

Tension crept over her shoulders. The man seemed to find fault in everything she did lately. The male gas company employee looked at her funny, and she missed two days of work because Scott locked her in the house. A wrong number on her cell phone caused him to drag her along on business in the middle of the night because he claimed she was untrustworthy.

It was during those night errands that she learned the truth about the man she lived with, had thought she'd fallen in love with while in college. He was secure, attentive, and paid her more attention than any college-age guy she knew. If only she'd been smart enough to see past his lies before everything changed.

A car alarm blared somewhere in the distance. She picked up her pace, jogging across the lot. The last time she'd arrived home late, Scott threatened to make her quit her job. It was important that she follow his rules, because her job was the only thing keeping her from being entirely dependent on him. Someday, maybe she'd work up the courage to ask one of the two attorneys she worked for to help her get away from him.

It was getting harder to ignore the fact that all her suspicions were true. Scott Carson was the main supplier for the heroin in the area. He also had a team of men who'd do anything he ordered, including killing her if she didn't drive him to do it himself.

There was no way he'd allow her to leave. She knew too much, and she was afraid his threats would come true. She wasn't ready to lie down and let him take her life.

An engine revved along the street, and she turned. The sight of the shiny metal emblem on the hood of the car as it turned into the parking lot paralyzed her with fear. She was blinded from the headlights aimed at her and growing closer, and as her flight response kicked in, she sprinted the last thirty feet to her vehicle.

She plowed into the side of the Duster, scrambling around the front bumper to the driver's door. Adrenaline shaking her body, she grasped the handle and yanked. She muffled her scream and looked around on the ground. Somewhere in the lot, she'd dropped her keys.

She lifted her gaze, hoping she had enough time to run back, but it was too late. *Shit. Shit. Shit.*

Scott rolled out of the backseat of the Mercedes, followed by two of the many men he had at his disposal. She slipped her hand into her purse, pushing her wallet, sunglasses, and makeup bag to the side, searching for her cell phone. If she could push 911, maybe there was a chance she could stall him until help arrived.

"Do you know what time it is?" Scott approached her.

The short brown hair she used to love to comb her fingers through made his sharp nose look even more angled. She ran her thumb over the keypad, counting the buttons on her cell. At one time, she'd found him striking and regal looking.

A head taller than she, he'd looked down that nose at her too many times for her to find him handsome anymore. She swallowed hard, knowing whatever she said or how many times she tried to explain that when her boss asked her to stay late, she was going to be later than normal getting home.

"I'm sorry," she whispered.

Scott's hand shot out and grasped her neck, shoving her against the car. She dropped her purse and grabbed for his wrist, unable to breathe. Lifted off her feet, she kicked her legs, trying to knock him off balance to take the excruciating pressure off her neck.

He pressed his lips against the side of her head. "What did I tell you I would do if you fuck around on me?"

She tried to shake her head, but his grip tightened. The outer corners of her vision darkened, and she struggled to draw air into her closed throat. Her gaze darted to the two men standing yards away, securing the area, and silently pleaded for their help.

They ignored her. She was only their boss's girlfriend, the troublemaker. She'd overheard Scott threaten to kill them on many occasions if they looked, spoke, or thought about her, and going by their reaction, she believed he'd do it too.

Welcoming the darkness that followed, she stopped struggling because she knew she'd pass out at any second, and she'd be able to ignore what was happening to her. Pain shot up her knees and elbows, and the solid ground gave no cushion to her tender body. She blinked, rolling to her side. Scott's oxfords landed in front of her face, and she realized he'd dropped her to the asphalt in front of him. She coughed, gasping in air. Her throat burned and her whole body screamed from the abuse.

Scott's foot lifted. She squeezed her eyes closed, steeling herself. Blunt force knocked her sideways at the same time her breath escaped and a piercing pain shot through her midsection. She drew her knees to her chest to block any more kicks but wasn't fast enough. He stomped on her ribs, rolling her over under the force of his blow.

Scott squatted down, grabbing her hair, and shoved a pistol in her cheek. "Open your mouth, bitch. You know the rules. The only person you answer to is me."

She clamped her lips together and shook her head but grew light-headed and had to breathe. She gasped, sucking in air. Scott shoved the barrel of the gun into her opened mouth. She moaned as the steel clanked against her teeth. Hyperventilating, she stilled, afraid she'd finally pissed him off and he was going to kill her.

He'd threatened it many times over the last two years. At first, she talked him out of his anger, asking him to forgive her for whatever he imagined she'd done wrong. Then she'd retreated when the demands reached a level that was untenable. The most she could do was grovel and beg his forgiveness, promising she'd try harder.

"As of right now, you no longer have a job. You won't take a piss without asking me for permission first." Scott pulled back the cocking mechanism without removing the gun from her mouth. "And if you even *think* about telling anyone or asking one of those fucking attorneys for help, you're dead. Do you hear me?"

He jabbed the pistol in farther, knocking against her molars, causing her jaw to clamp down in reflex. She squeezed her eyes shut against the agony at the same time her upper body went in a different direction, and an intense piercing pain took the air from her lungs.

She mumbled around the gun, pleading for her life. Scott spit on her face. "Let's see how bad you want to live. If you make it home on your own, I won't kill you…this time. But if for some reason you don't show up in an hour, I'll make a phone call to one of my men who'll be following you. And then…well, you know what happens next, don't you?"

Then the gun was gone and someone tossed her keys onto her chest. A few seconds later, a car engine roared to life and drove away, leaving her alone. She lay on the ground, unable to draw enough air into her lungs. Something was seriously wrong this time. She cried out as she moved her arm to feel her side, positive her hand would come away bloody. But there was no wound, only the worst pain she'd ever experienced.

She prayed for what seemed like hours, but no one came to her rescue. Her body soon shook from cold, which hurt but motivated her to try to get into her car. Hunched over, she held her ribs, sure that they were broken. It was impossible to inhale or exhale in more than short puffs. She clung to the side of her Duster to keep on her feet.

A police cruiser sped by with lights and sirens blaring. She slid into the driver's seat. Exhausted, aching everywhere, and light-headed, she sat there with her eyes closed. Scott had too much power and too many men working for him for her to think she could get away tonight.

He'd often bragged about having connections in the police force, to eliminate her places to run. She dug her fingers into her purse, pulling out the few receipts she'd folded perfectly and kept in the side pouch. Carefully, she unfolded them all until she found what she was looking for.

Hidden among the old grocery receipts was a small piece of paper with a phone number on it. Tears rolled down her cheeks unchecked as she folded her lifeline back up and hid it in her purse. She'd never found the courage to call, but having that piece of paper gave her hope that someday she wouldn't be living the life that she'd made for herself.

She wasn't stupid, no matter what Scott thought.

She had to get away, but that wasn't happening tonight. No, she'd wait until her ribs healed and she had enough strength to plan her escape better. This time she'd succeed.

She started the car and backed out of the parking spot. Once she made it home, she'd grow stronger and prepare for Scott to come after her again. If she had to kill him, then so be it.

About the Author

Top-selling romance author Debra Kayn lives with her family at the foot of the Bitterroot Mountains in beautiful Idaho. She enjoys riding motorcycles, playing tennis, fishing, and creating chaos for the men in the garage.

Her love of family ties and laughter makes her a natural to write heartwarming contemporary stories to the delight of her readers. Oh, let's cut to the chase. She loves to write about real men and the women who love them.

When Debra was nineteen years old, a man kissed her without introducing himself. When they finally came up for air, the first words out of his mouth were *Will you have my babies?* Considering Debra's weakness for a sexy, badass man who is strong enough to survive her attitude, she said yes. A quick wedding at the House of Amour and four babies later, she's living her own unbelievable romance book.